Ties That Inspire

John Hagan

Goose River Press
Waldoboro, Maine

Copyright © 2016 John Hagan

All rights reserved. With the exception of quotations drawn from classical sources, no part of this book may be reproduced or transmitted in any form without permission from the publisher.

PUBLISHER'S NOTE

Ties That Inspire is a collection of short stories. Exclusive of historical figures, other nationally prominent individuals, and documented events or factual locations; the names, characters, places, and incidents portrayed herein are fictitious. Any similarity to actual persons (living or deceased), events, or locations is coincidental or inferred.

Library of Congress Control Card Number: 2016939514

ISBN: 978-1-59713-170-4

Fifth Printing, 2019

Front Cover Photo by Deborah A. Hagan
Back Cover Photo by N. Jean Hagan

Published by
Goose River Press
3400 Friendship Road
Waldoboro, Maine 05472
www.gooseriverpress.com

Special Thanks

Joseph Gural and Donald Justice,
whose suggestions provided the seminal ideas
for three stories.
Carolyn Gravelle, whose anecdote inspired
a humorous exchange in one of the stories.

Contents

Also by John Hagan

An Irish View of the Country

A Long Farewell

"Bucolic Images"
(*Goose River Anthology, 2014*)

"An Old Friend Called"
(*Goose River Anthology, 2012*)

"Saddle Pals"
(*Goose River Anthology, 2010*)

"Vanishing Country"
(*Goose River Anthology, 2007*)

Ties That Inspire

I am firm in my belief that
A teacher lives on and on
Through his students.
Good teaching is forever
And the teacher is immortal.

—The Thread that Runs So True
Jesse Stuart

As my lovely date and I sat in the audience of Boardwalk Hall in Atlantic City on that warm September evening, I was struck by the substantial difference in the responses of the first four contestants from that of the fifth and last. The master of ceremonies, Bert Parks, had asked each of the five finalists for the crown of Miss America what person had been most inspirational in her life and for what reasons. Given the pageant year's relative proximity to three national luminaries' untimely and violent deaths, they were aptly and predictably cited by three of the finalists as being profoundly influential. Miss Maine spoke of John F. Kennedy and his spirit of national service and optimism. Miss Colorado delineated the inspiration she derived from Martin Luther King's indefatigable pursuit of his dream for black America. Miss Wisconsin practically wept as she described the strength she drew from the zest for life and zeal for justice that abounded in Robert F. Kennedy. Drawing upon a more historic and international figure, Miss Ohio found motivation in the courage and resolve of Joan of Arc, and the Buckeye beauty deftly supported her choice of the French heroine with a quote from Mark Twain: "She is easily and by far the most extraordinary person the human race has ever produced."* When the fifth finalist, Miss Kentucky, cited her choice for an abidingly influential person, the nearly palpable shock that rippled across the large audience practically shouted that she had made a careless personal choice.

"For me," said Mary Beth Adkins, "Miss Hessie Pennix stands as the most admirable and humane person I know, and without her I would not be competing here tonight."

The crowd, of course, had no idea who Hessie Pennix was and likely wondered if Miss Kentucky had decided to concede the crown by naming such an insignificant personality, but I knew the reasons for Mary Beth's thoughtful albeit risky selection. Miss Hester Pennix was a living legend in the area around the tiny town of Fisty in the Appalachian Mountain region of Knott County, Kentucky.

Miss Hessie, as she was affectionately known, was a graduate of Centre College in Danville, Kentucky, and she had emigrated after graduation from her home in Louisville to the mountains of Knott County. Fresh from college with a teaching credential, she had responded to an announcement sent to Centre, stating the need for "a modestly paid 1-12 teacher for the children in the area of Fisty, Kentucky." The actual remuneration for the position made "modestly paid" one of the most colossal hyperboles in the history of recruiting legerdemain.

Hester Elinore Pennix moved into a second-floor bedroom of a boarding house in Fisty in August of 1922. Born the fourth child into a family of eight children in Louisville in 1901, her father was a mathematics professor at the University of Louisville, and her mother was a full-time parent and part-time seamstress. Uncommonly bright and unusually tall, the svelte and auburn-haired Hester had won a full scholarship to the prestigious Centre College at seventeen, and most of her instructors and classmates at the college assumed that when she graduated with a dual major in English and mathematics, she would accept the fellowship extended to her for master's work at Harvard University.

Miss Kentucky used her brief response time to provide the general reasons for her choice of Hessie Pennix: kindness, tenacity, generosity, altruism, and pedagogy. Naturally, Miss Kentucky's time limits restricted any expansion upon the contributions to Fisty, Kentucky that made Miss Hessie so noteworthy, but those who came of age near that Eastern Kentucky town knew them well.

I was a skinny six-year-old when I joined the other students in the one-room schoolhouse situated near old-growth woods and reached by a sparsely graveled road that ran east and west out of Fisty. I had three other "classmates," two boys and a girl, and our arrival that September for first grade augmented the aggregate school population to 39 pupils, ranging from grades one through twelve. I had already heard plenty about Miss Hessie from my three older brothers, one of whom was in the eighth grade and one in the ninth. My oldest brother, Randy, had dropped out after tenth grade to join my dad in a nearby coalmine.

Miss Hessie was well into her long career by the time I showed up with my lunch pail and book bag, and she bore a reputation as both a tough taskmaster and a consummate humanitarian. That reputation was not built upon hearsay.

The Great Depression that ravaged the nation through the thirties and early forties was especially hard on those around Fisty who knew stark privation as a way of life. Hessie's meager salary would fluctuate according to the economic times, but being the resourceful teacher she was, she not only made do with what she had but managed to provide assistance to a number of her destitute students. In the late nineteen-twenties she purchased a dilapidated bungalow at the edge of town, and with her own elbow grease and the assistance of townspeople, she was able to reconstitute the house into a charming refuge for her evenings of reading and baking. During the school months, Hessie would often bake biscuits during the nights before class days and bring them and a jar of honey to school for the children who often went without breakfast. Hessie made herself available to the families around Fisty in many ways, including visiting the sick, helping in the fields, and volunteering with the Red Cross. Quite attractive in her younger years, she had a number of suitors, but no relationship reached an engagement or marriage, and when questioned about having her own children, her standard reply was that she had a schoolroom full of them.

To me Miss Hessie gave no quarter, and from me she accepted no lame excuses for incomplete homework or slipshod class work. She obviously saw something in me I would likely have never seen in myself, and as I progressed through the grade levels, she relentlessly imposed more and more exasperating and sophisticated writing assignments upon me. I often bridled at her expectations, noting that my composition topics were more complex than those she gave pupils two or three years my senior. As I advanced in my education, I began to suspect some method to her madness, and while I never relished her challenges, I resolved to beat her at her own game. I began to accept her assignments as gauntlets I would take up to make her cease and desist in my weekly torments. I was, however, the victim of my own successes, as they only increased the difficulty of my assignments.

The dictionary she lent me became my six-gun in our little duel, and although she frequently noted my "bigworditis," she seemed to applaud my efforts to expand my compositional horizons. By eleventh grade I was actually attempting some short stories and essays on my own, and I would proffer them for her perusal. Never the gusher, her slightest affirmation was grist for my further attempts, and by the beginning of my twelfth grade, she had me dreaming of college as an English or journalism major. Assisting me in my application, Miss Hessie's recommendation letter resulted in my admission to Vanderbilt University, and her cosigning of loans from the local bank helped to meet tuition expenses. I am now a syndicated writer, living in New York City. Were it not for Miss Hessie, I would likely be working today in the coalmines with my three brothers where my father contracted his fatal pneumoconiosis or black lung disease.

As I began my eighth year of studies, five first-graders entered our school, and of the two little boys and three little girls, a towheaded darling with a recently lost first tooth was among them. Her name was Mary Beth Adkins, and notwithstanding my indifference to the younger children, I took note of Miss Hessie's extraordinary attentions to her. Indeed, Mary Beth was a charmer although retiring and reticent. Keeping daily tabs on Miss Hessie's efforts with Mary Beth, I could not help making comparisons to the demands upon the new student's development that were much the same as those she made upon me. Progressing through my high school studies, I became increasingly intrigued by the alacrity with which Mary Beth mastered her studies and the ease with which she emerged from her retiring persona.

Graduation, of course, took me to college in Nashville, Tennessee. My classes there as a dual major in English and journalism were most demanding and often frustrating. I was not only cast into a pool of competitors that included the most elite young scholars in the country, but my empirical knowledge of the world had been severely limited by my Appalachian origins. In fact, my classroom contributions often betrayed a provincialism that was juxtaposed with the *savoir-faire* of those who had arrived at Vanderbilt from exclusive prep schools and culturally enriched experiences that were often enhanced by international travel.

While many of my classmates at Vanderbilt traveled abroad or gained experience in family practices or businesses during summer months, I returned to Fisty at the end of each winter term to earn as much as possible as a hired hand on Knott County farms. Naturally, I would spend a great deal of time with Miss Hessie, sharing my collegiate experiences and discussing my career hopes. During these interludes, I would also have the opportunity to talk with Mary Beth Atkins, who as a junior high-aged girl was already becoming a rare beauty and demonstrating impressive intellect. Miss Hessie so doted upon her that when the girl dropped by her teacher's house while I was there, I became for my mentor a part of the woodwork. I felt no slight by Hessie's fascination with Mary Beth because I was equally captivated.

Graduating from Vanderbilt, I took a series of jobs as a beat writer for small broadsheets in the South before talking my way into a major newspaper in the East and launching a syndicated column. During that time I maintained periodic correspondence with Miss Hessie, who continued to provide steadfast and stalwart instruction for her pupils in Fisty.

By the time Mary Beth had reached high school age, teenagers from one-room schoolhouses were traveling by bus to the Knott County High School in Hindman. Mary Beth was becoming increasingly adroit at mathematics under Hessie's personal tutelage, and she would annually score among the top students in Kentucky in state scholarship testing. Traveling to Eastern Kentucky University to take the Scholastic Aptitude Test, she posted a 760 on the math component of the test in the spring of her junior year. Although she earned a full scholarship for mathematics studies at Miami University in Oxford, Ohio that covered tuition, books, and room and board, her family's financial state could not provide for personal expenses. Again, Miss Hessie was at the ready, subsidizing Mary Beth's incidentals and travel costs. While an undergrad at Miami, Mary Beth competed in several Kentucky beauty contests, and with a naturally melodic voice, she honed her skills as an *a cappella* soloist. She progressed in her poise and presentation, eventually capturing the crown of Miss Kentucky in the competition that led to the

Miss America Pageant.

Graduating *cum laude* from Miami University and selected to Phi Beta Kappa, Mary Beth accepted a fellowship with stipend to the Georgia Institute of Technology for her master's degree in mathematics, but she also had the challenge of the Miss America competition. Processing with relative ease through the rigors of the various performances, she found herself among the five finalists for the coveted crown.

I, in the meantime, had been following Mary Beth's career as I pursued my own with an almost obsessive dedication. Folks back home alerted me to her successes, and I was well aware that she was competing for Miss America. Meeting deadlines was hectic, and I rarely had time for a social life. My romantic relationships with women were nearly always subordinate to my work, a phenomenon that made those relationships typically short-lived. Nevertheless, I longed to see Mary Beth's performance in person, so I wheedled two prime seats from a journalist friend with connections. For something this spectacular, however, I wanted a date with a beautiful woman. I had not talked to the one I preferred in nearly a year, and I was most apprehensive about asking her. She accepted my offer graciously, although reminding me that I had been negligent in my calls and attentions. I arranged for her flight to New York, and together we drove to Atlantic City, New Jersey.

Atlantic City was frenetic and celebratory, and negotiating traffic was a tedious exercise in orienteering, but at length we reached Boardwalk Hall. My date raised a number of questions about Miss Kentucky, and she was seemingly more curious about her than she was interested in me.

Completing their responses to Bert Parks' question, the five finalists were sent back stage while the judges pondered and discussed their voting. The hall was alive with the crowd's discussions and theories on who would be the next Miss America. For my own part, I was so anxious for Mary Beth that I could hardly make small talk with my date who had become completely taken with the glamour and glitz of her surroundings.

After what seemed liked hours, Parks returned to the microphone and summoned the five finalists to center stage. Displaying apparent composure, each was surely wild with anxiety. The master of ceremonies first explained the dynamics of the outcome, citing the responsibilities of the first runner-up should Miss America be unable to perform her duties. As was the protocol of the proceedings, Parks began the countdown to the Miss America crown with nerve-racking deliberation. "Fourth runner-up for the title of Miss America is...Miss Colorado!" The audience responded in polite applause, knowing that Miss Colorado would likely be privately crushed. Receiving her flowers, she stepped to the side of Parks. "Third runner-up...Miss Wisconsin!" Again, an almost sympathetic applause ensued, and Miss Wisconsin gracefully accepted her judgment and flowers and tactfully stepped aside. "Second runner-up...Miss Maine!" As an Eastern Seaboard representative, Miss Maine seemed to gain an even more enthusiastic and empathetic applause. A hush fell over the hall, as the *denouement* had arrived. The next announcement would by elimination identify the new Miss America. Parks oozed theatrically as he restated the importance of the second-place contestant. "And now ladies and gentlemen, I give you the first runner-up for Miss America, who, as I have said, will fulfill the duties of Miss America if she is unable to do so. First runner-up...Miss Kentucky!" The applause for Mary Beth quickly melded into that for Miss Ohio, the new Miss America.

Mary Beth Adkins turned to Miss Ohio and courteously congratulated her before the other three finalists joined her. Crowned by the previous year's winner, the new Miss America commenced her victory promenade on the runway as Parks began his signature song: "There she is, Miss America. There she is, your ideal...."

My heart went out to Mary Beth, even though her experience was so singular that legions of young women in America would likely have ached for her opportunity. I was resolved to talk to her backstage, and after appealing to an event official's sentimentality regarding my hometown connection with Miss Kentucky, he conducted my date and me to the area where the contestants had assembled after the ceremony.

When Mary Beth saw us, she burst into tears, not from disappointment but from exquisite joy. She virtually sailed around and through the assembly and greeted Miss Hessie Pennix, who engulfed her in her arms in such a maternal way that it nearly silenced all discourse in the room. Practically everyone divined at once that the woman in whose embrace Mary Beth was wrapped was her life's inspiration.

Mary Beth had many obligations that night and had limited time with us. Coming so close to the Miss America crown only to fall tantalizingly short was obviously painful, but knowing that the paragon of humanity, who had taken her so far in her still very young life and who had imbued in her a reverence for her roots, was present to see her on this special night was the balm of disappointment. While I felt briefly like a fifth wheel in our reunion, Mary Beth turned and thanked me in such an emotive manner that I inferred an appreciation not only for bringing Miss Hessie but in rekindling ties that traced themselves to a remarkable woman and a humble schoolhouse in Fisty, Kentucky.

In spite of periodic updates about her from lifelong friends in Fisty, I all but lost track of Mary Beth over time. Nine years after the pageant, Miss Hester Pennix slept away in her reading chair in the bungalow that had become symbolic of her kindness, wisdom, and pedagogy. A dog-eared copy of Charlotte Bronte's *Jane Eyre* lay in her lap.

Attending Miss Hessie's funeral along with a host of others, I encountered a breathtaking blond who was now Dr. Mary Beth Adkins, professor of finite mathematics at Northwestern University. She had touched me on the arm at the gravesite and said, "Long time, no see!"

Eschewing the crush of humanity assembled at the community center after the funeral, Mary Beth and I had lunch together at the Koffee Kup in town. When she mentioned that she was still unmarried, I queried tastelessly and tongue-in-cheek, "You're not gonna be another Hessie Pennix, are ya?"

Wryly, she answered, "I should be so honored, but if the right guy came along..."

Finishing her thought with a Cheshire-cat smile, I bargained, "I may just know the perfect gent."

[*]"Saint Joan of Arc" essay, 1904

Significant Moments

When we fully understand the brevity of life,
Its fleeting joys and unavoidable pains;
When we accept the facts that all men and women
Are approaching an inevitable doom:
The consciousness of it should make us
More kindly and considerate of each other.

—*The Myth of the Soul*
Clarence Darrow

Sitting in the last pew near the middle aisle of Saint Theresa of the Little Flower Church on that raw and overcast January day, I watched in guilt and sadness as Devon Finley's ashes were borne in an urn by his brother toward the altar. Devon's frail and aged mother, Mairead; his four other siblings; and his twelve nieces and nephews formed a somber procession behind Sean. Sitting in the last pew on the other side of the middle aisle was Devon's and my mutual friend, Conall Burke, and the two of us exchanged facial expressions of regret and accountability. The funeral Mass was sparsely attended, as most of Devon's former friends, classmates, and associates had long before said good-bye to him successively in a discordant or antagonistic manner.

Attending the same Catholic grade school and high school, Devon, Conall, and I came of age together. Owing to their superior grades and family finances, they were able to attend and graduate from the prestigious Ignatius University in Southern Ohio, but I attended the less selective and more affordable Aquinas College in Northern Kentucky.

John T. Hagan

In some ways Devon's was an ugly duckling story, his being in both junior- and senior-high years rather gangly and uncoordinated. Adding to a moderate clumsiness in his pre and early teenage years was the continuing pain he felt in his right leg from ankle to knee. When, as a ten-year-old, Devon had been crossing a busy street after departing a city transit bus on his way home from school, a bread truck ran a red light and struck him. The snub-nosed vehicle dragged him between its front bumper and left wheel for nearly a city block before eyewitnesses could alert the oblivious and delinquent driver. After several surgeries and skin grafts performed by local specialists and a huge settlement paid by the bread company, Devon walked limp-free again in his mid teens.

By our senior year at Saint Aloysius Preparatory, Devon had stretched to 6'3", but he probably was not a pound over 180. During that year, he, Conall, and I commenced the roguish era of our camaraderie. This span of kindred spirit was largely the result of a nascent wildness that was now manifest in part by Saturday morning daredevil rides in Conall's shrewdly negotiated, two-door, powder-blue Oldsmobile with rusted rocker panels, full-wheel hubcaps, reflector-studded mud flaps, and a salacious spinner knob displaying the "talents" of a scantily-clad temptress. Exceeding 90-miles-per-hour down Shiloh Springs Road in the Olds that Conall whimsically called the *Mayflower* because in his total fantasy "many a little Puritan had come across," we would hit the hump in the road created by the intersecting state route and go airborne for fifteen feet before slamming to Earth with a thud that nearly ruptured the 7.70 x 15" threadbare whitewalls. We gave up the madness when I almost lost my kneecaps on the dashboard one Saturday.

Although Devon and Conall were the sons of prosperous family-practice physicians, I rarely felt socially inferior because of my "shanty Irish" family's residence in a two-bedroom bungalow, where I lived with my parents and two brothers. My father's highest earning year was $7,200.00 in 1967, an annual income that would have been pocket change to Devon and Conall's fathers.

As the three of us processed through undergraduate schools, I by fits and starts, Devon and Conall began to look very much the finished young men. Conall, at 6'2", had always had some meat on him, but Devon had begun to broaden at the shoulders and add an adult weight that not only enhanced his frame but also gave to his previously narrow face a breadth that was now turning the head of many a comely coed. Although Devon was a pre-med major and Conall a history major, both had benefited from their fathers' influence, and they secured part-time positions as lab technicians in the Hematology Laboratory at Saint Ursula's Hospital during their sophomore year at nearby Ignatius. At Saint Ursula's, Devon was becoming an understood favorite among some of the student nurses, and during summer months he would arrive for his night-crew duties after a day of sun tanning at the country club and charm the budding Florence Nightingales with his white lab shirt and bronzed arms and face.

By the end of my sophomore year at Aquinas, I was in dire need of money to meet my junior- and senior-year tuitions, so I prevailed upon Conall to intercede on my behalf with the lab supervisor at Saint Ursula's to add me to the five pre-med students who were about to begin a paid six-week, summer orientation program in hematology work. They would subsequently serve as lab technicians in the evenings, weekends, and holidays during their junior and senior years at Ignatius. Notwithstanding my biology and chemistry deficiencies as an English major, I was added to the group and completed the program, but I was clearly the "anchor man" in this class of accomplished science majors.

The fun was about to begin.

Since it was an easy run from Aquinas College, I was often able to hop into my dilapidated Ford and drive to Saint

John T. Hagan

Ursula's Hospital to work a Friday-night shift running complete blood counts and urinalyses for pre-operation patients. I would then assist the Saturday and Sunday day crews by drawing blood from the medical-floor patients and running CBC's in the lab. During our junior year at Ignatius and Aquinas, Devon, Conall, and I pursued student nurses at Saint Ursula's with a religious zeal, but most regarded us as simply bothersome and clueless. Devon, however, was becoming something of a catch, working as he was toward medical school at The Ohio State University.

Somehow the three of us convinced the lab supervisor that we should all be excused from duties during the week of our spring breaks, and we piled into the beautiful red Chevy convertible Devon's dad had bought him in the fall and flew low down I-75 to Fort Lauderdale, Florida. Making the typical beginners' mistake, we walked the beach for the entire first day and spent most of the remaining days in our room with severe sunburns at the Camelot Motel off Atlantic Boulevard, suffering the wages of our impetuosity. On Friday, however, we willed ourselves down to the Elbow Room, famous from its role in the movie *Where the Boys Are*, and we met and sparked three fetching teachers from Cleveland. Leaving for Ohio the next day, we had little time to make serious inroads, but the more troublesome detail was that we were 20 and they 25.

The first weekend after classes had resumed in early April, Conall decided that we should pay a surprise visit to our "girl friends" from Lauderdale who lived together in a duplex in a Cleveland suburb. We found replacements for our weekend lab assignments and bolted for Shaker Heights in our shorts and T-shirts with the top down on Devon's convertible. As we drove north, we discovered that our "mistake on the lake" was that Cuyahoga County at night is dramatically colder in April than daytime temps in Southern Ohio. Although our three sirens greeted us graciously, we discovered by degrees that our odyssey should have been given greater forethought. We had, of course, lied to these ladies in Florida about our ages, so when they mentioned their Friday-night barhopping routine, the jig was nearly up. They had, however, already been exchanging furtive glances at the naïve nature of our exchanges. The great axe fell on our impostor necks when four burly construction workers arrived at the house to join the ladies for drinks. We suddenly remembered that we had a long drive home, and, stammering our excuses, we departed freezing Cleveland, wearing shorts and T-shirts in snow flurries and a 30-degree temperature. No doubt, the teacher ladies and hardhat gents had many laughs at our expense over husky mugs of Budweiser.

Of singular note in Devon's casting a wide net in student-nurse flirtations was the curious attention he was paying in April and May to a striking senior student who was completing her three-year program in June. Tall and beautiful, Madeleine Hastings carried herself with a bearing suggesting that she would not dally with fools. The field-playing Devon was smitten. His overtures to Madeleine did not, however, lie entirely fallow, as the walls gradually came down in her defenses, and by her graduation, she and Devon could be found together at the country club pool, high-end restaurants, and numerous social events. So taken with Madeleine was Devon that Conall observed to me, "I think the designated stud-muffin has been led from the pasture."

While at Aquinas, I had taken up tennis in my free time, and by the summer after my junior year, I was skilled enough to enter local tournaments with some expectation of advancing past the first round if I had not drawn a seeded player immediately. As such, I was playing a third-round match in the county tournament in August, but with my clunker Ford in the shop for repairs, Devon had driven me to the courts and departed. Leaving the court after a thrashing from the second seed, I found Devon waiting for me as expected in the parking lot. What was not expected was that he was there in his red Chevy with the top down, and sitting practically in his lap was a gorgeously tanned blond in terrycloth top and shorts that I knew as one Madeleine Hastings. To say I was awestruck would be classic understatement. Still sweating from my annihilation on the court, I pushed in beside Madeleine on the bench seat, and her fragrant perfume and prepossessing presence intoxicated me. When they dropped me off at my home, I watched Devon and Madeleine drive away, and for the first time in my life, I felt the very sobering reality of my station. They were F. Scott Fitzgerald's Buchanans, and I lived in Charles Dickens's Tom-All-Alone's.

Owing to his lofty grade-point average at Ignatius, fortified by A's in both semesters of organic chemistry labs and lectures, Devon was accepted to The Ohio State University Medical School after only three years of an undergraduate program. Completing one year of med school at Ohio State, he would receive his Bachelor of Science from Ignatius. With Devon off to O.S.U. in the fall, Madeleine began her career as a graduate nurse in her nearby hometown while awaiting the results of state boards that would soon qualify her to practice as a registered nurse. Devon, however, pining away, returned every weekend to be with Madeleine, a pattern that was inimical to the nearly 24-7 demands of his program. Although he eked out passing grades at Ohio State and qualified for a bachelor's degree from Ignatius, his future as a physician had ended. Madeleine, during this time, had resumed a high school relationship that would blossom into romance and put an end to any life with Devon.

At the end of my first year of high school teaching and during Devon's first year as a sales representative for a pharmaceutical company, we traveled to Las Cruces, New Mexico to join Conall after his first year as a grad student at New Mexico State University. We flew to El Paso, Texas and then bus-rode to Las Cruces to enjoy seven halcyon days of fun-filled travel from the N.M.S.U. campus to Redondo Beach, California; Las Vegas, Nevada; the Hoover Dam; and the

Grand Canyon before returning home to Ohio. (Actually, we never reached the Grand Canyon because the water pump in Conall's maroon Ford convertible gave up the ghost about fifty miles short of the big crevice.) Conall had a few residual responsibilities attendant to his assistantship, so we remained in Las Cruces for two of our nine days of adventure. Returning from the university to his rented bungalow around 10:00 a.m. on the second day, Conall decided we should take a day-hike over to one of the Organ Mountains beyond the nearby "A" Mountain, so named for the New Mexico State Aggies. Be it known that university officials routinely issued stern warnings to students and staff to avoid the very kind of lunacy in the desert we planned.

Purchasing canteens at a local Army surplus store, we headed out on foot at about 11:15 a.m. to walk "over to that mountain" we had decided to climb. At about 2:30 p.m., we were now walking with nearly empty canteens "over to that mountain" that was seemingly no closer than it was at 11:15. At about three o'clock, we stumbled upon the rotting carcass of a horned Hereford that looked like he had planned a similar adventure. Needless to say, the wisdom of the university officials was now crystallizing in our sun-addled brains. Reaching the inspired conclusion that commencing a return trip was absolutely crucial at that moment, we turned and headed in what we thought was a direct route to the campus. By about 6:00 p.m., we had wandered to a gravel road that took us back to the university and, as we later discovered, would have allowed us to drive almost to the foot of our mountain objective. We hit the local convenience store and bought a sack of ice and two six-packs of sixteen-ounce Pepsis that we nearly drained in an hour.

After our daytime survival test in the desert, we decided to reward ourselves with a night on the town across the border in Juarez, Mexico. Accosted and fleeced in a second-floor restaurant by three B-girls for whom we were accused of buying the drinks they were ordering in Spanish, we angrily paid the tab and left. Emboldened by several Tequilas we had swilled in a seedy saloon down the street, we decided to exact our pound of flesh from the manager who had demanded hefty payment for drinks that were likely water, so we returned to the restaurant and ordered the most expensive entrées on the menu. Waiting until the orders had likely been processed, we bolted down the back steps with the manager cursing and threatening us in Spanish. We ran hell-bent-for-leather to the border office and calmly slipped our remaining coins into the turnstile slots, careful to give no reason for suspicion to the guards. During the drive back to Las Cruces, Conall regaled Devon and me with horror stories of Aggie grad students who had found themselves in the Juarez jail for similar high jinks.

Our desert and Juarez exploits were just two of many that interspersed our checkered history together (freezing our asses off one night in a roadside ditch, while attempting a Bobby Kennedy-inspired 75-mile walk, being another), but our friendship endured and flourished, not because of any monumental or triumphant experiences together but because they enriched us with the vicissitudes of life. Alas, "Moonlight" Graham's sage observation in *Field of Dreams* is so true, however, because we did not recognize the most significant moments in our lives while they were happening.

The three of us would, of course, eventually take separate paths while remaining in touch when possible. As an ROTC graduate from Ignatius, Conall entered the United States Army as a second lieutenant after grad school, and he was the giddy winner of an all-expense-paid, twelve-month vacation in the Mekong Delta during his two-year service requirement. I would marry in my mid 20's, Conall in his early 30's, and Devon in his late 30's. Over the years, Conall and I noticed an increasing jaundice in Devon's bearing and in his remarks about other friends. His personality was changing for the worse. Always the fabricator with a penchant for bilious hyperbole, Devon's advancing practice of rank mendac-

ity went without remark among his other friends and associates, for a time. At length, however, his bile and lies took
their toll on most of his relationships, including those with
Conall and me. His marriage had gone horribly sour within
six months, and after some very ugly domestic episodes, it
ended abruptly in a rancorous divorce. Although we heard
from a number of sources that Devon had either been fired
from or quit various jobs and would live during the interims
on the money from his childhood accident, Conall and I had
terminated our contact with him and, like others, ignored
him.

Many years later, my wife and I were hosting a pre-
Christmas party at our house for her family. In what was my
absolute busiest of moments serving and engaging a house-
ful of guests, my daughter pulled me aside and said that
Devon Finley was on the telephone and needed to speak to
me at once. Not having talked to or seen Devon since our
early forties, I was provoked that he would insist on speaking
with me after my daughter told him I was hosting a family
party.

Devon said that he was about to be dismissed as a
patient from Saint Ursula's Hospital and that he had no one
to drive him home. He claimed that he had cancer and that
parts of his feet had been amputated. The truth, as I later
learned, was that he had lost toes on both feet from his mid-
life development of Type 2 Diabetes, exacerbated by his
heavy drinking. I told him that I was simply not available at
that time, and he allowed that if he could locate his wallet,
he would take a cab. I assured him that I would call him
soon and make arrangements to visit him at his house. The
next day, I called Conall and described what had transpired,
and he agreed to drive over from Muncie, Indiana, where he
was teaching at Ball State University, and accompany me to
Devon's house the following day, Christmas Eve. Conall was
adamant, however, that he would make the visit most reluctantly, as Devon had lied to him all too often.

John T. Hagan

When Devon opened his front door, the fetid breath of what was once an elegant Colonial-style home belched out at us before we entered the foyer. He greeted us in squalor, and we walked over floors strewn with putrescent food and streaked with dried blood. Hobbling badly, he led us on bloodied and gauze-wrapped feet into a den, furnished only with a tattered sofa and two upholstered but badly soiled stuffed chairs. The filthy carpeting reeked of spilled whiskey, and the sliding glass door leading to a patio had been breeched with a baseball-sized hole that suggested the work of a vandal. Small shards of glass still lay in the carpeting by the tracking. Two pictures of dead men were the only wall decorations, one of which was of his physician father, Thomas Patrick Finley, and the other of his Irish hero, John Fitzgerald Kennedy. The scene would conjure for me Miss Havisham's dire and dreadful room in *Great Expectations*, and to a great extent, I shared Pip's reaction.

As he collapsed into one of the upholstered chairs, he asked if one of us would bring him a cola from the kitchen table, and he said to help ourselves to any beverages in the refrigerator. Conall made the run, and as he returned, he rolled his eyes at me in response to a kitchen scene that made the den look like a *Good Housekeeping* picture of order and cleanliness. We both declined any refreshments and settled in for a discussion of his infirmities. Devon, however, eschewed references to his condition and surprised us with the tone and topics of his conversation. He was quite upbeat and effusive, gesticulating wildly at times in his discussion of our bygone days and adventures. I daresay that a great deal of his animation was due to the high content of caffeine in his cola or to something more potent he had likely absorbed prior to our arrival.

At length, and after some rather indiscreet references to his ex-wife, Devon mused wistfully about the girls in his life. Almost as preamble to the focal point of his reminiscences, he made passing references to girls he had known in college and in the workplace. Eventually, however, he transitioned into a poignant narrative of the love of his life. She was, of course, Madeleine Hastings. He told us that while he was at Ohio State she had decided that for religious reasons she could not reconcile marriage to a Catholic. The tenets of Catholicism were simply too incompatible with her sect of Protestantism to allow for harmonious nuptials. He was sure, however, that Madeleine had simply fallen for another and was trying to soften the blow to him with obfuscation. He longed to see and talk to her again, not in any absurd hope of a rekindling a lost relationship but only to hear her voice and learn something of her life. At times, he seemed quite wounded and hurt, but for the most part he understood Madeleine's choice. What was most intriguing for Conall and me was his belief that his life would have been substantially more fulfilling and meaningful had Madeleine been integral to it.

Conall and I sat with Devon for about two hours until we needed to return home on Christmas Eve. Grasping our coat sleeves at the front door, he implored us to visit again soon, and we gave him our assurances of such. About two or three days after Christmas, he called me again and said that he had no will to live and that he intended to end his torment. Not taking him seriously, I urged him perfunctorily to hold on, and I promised that Conall and I would make regular visits after New Year's to clean his house and ready it for sale. We would help him find something more manageable and make sustained efforts to assist him.

After New Year's Day, I began calling Devon's house with no success in reaching him. Since he had told Conall and me that he would need additional surgeries during the new year, I concluded that he had been hospitalized again and that he would call me when he returned home. At about 11:30 p.m. on January 7th, I took a frightening call from the county coroner's office, asking if I knew a Devon Finley. Confirming that I did, I was told that Devon had been found by the police in a pool of blood in his den with a handgun in hand. Lying near him was a mobile phone and scrap of paper bearing my telephone number. A concerned neighbor had noticed a mail buildup and had contacted the police. Authorities calculated Devon's death as occurring on New Year's Day.

Over lunch after the funeral Mass, Conall and I discussed and lamented what might have become of Devon had we not abandoned him for many years. True, the loss of Madeleine was more devastating than we had known, and even marriage to a beautiful woman had not filled the void. No doubt, his ex-wife was unable to obviate his emotional attachment to Madeleine. Under any circumstances or for whatever reasons, what might have been for a highly intelligent and handsome young man resolved itself in an outcome of blood, filth, stench, and death many years later, and Conall and I could not ignore or deny our part in it.

The Bottle Farm

During the whole of a dull, dark and soundless day, [...]
When the clouds hung oppressively low in the heavens,
I had been passing [...] a [...] dreary tract of country;
And [...] found myself [near...] the [...] House of Usher.
With the first glimpse of the building,
A sense of insufferable gloom pervaded my spirit.

—The Fall of the House of Usher
Edgar Allen Poe

I was nine years old when I saw it, and while the passage of time has dulled some of my recollections, the Bottle Farm still holds dominion over the most graphic and eerie memories of my childhood.

As a then-college sophomore and strapping football player, my oldest brother was home for spring break in late March that year, and he had heard tell of a place known as a bottle farm. Seeking a day trip of interest, he resolved to take his girlfriend to the country to find it, and being pestered by me to join them, he acquiesced and allowed his garrulous brother to ride in the backseat. Although the warm spring weather and its blooms and blossoms were fast approaching on this overcast and dreary afternoon, the gusting breezes and dark clouds made the sixty-degree temperature disagreeable and chilling. We rode together in my dad's company car, a powder-blue four-door Plymouth, down Ohio Route 4 to the village of Farmersville, and once there my brother asked the locals if they knew of a bottle farm. Somewhat hesitant and oblique in their responses, the villagers pointed us in the general direction of this numinous place. Zigzagging along a number of narrow county roads, at length we turned on to a gravel byway and approached one of the strangest sites any of us had ever seen. Seemingly inspired by an ancient culture's burial grounds, the Bottle Farm captivated us while we were still in our car.

My brother's date urged him to keep driving past this foreboding acreage, but he ignored her petitions and turned into a muddy lane leading to a fascinating barnyard. With his date waiting anxiously in the car, my brother and I stepped on to the grounds and surveyed our surroundings. Although the sorely neglected but most intriguing Victorian house with wraparound porch seemed unoccupied, the barn seized our immediate interest. It was at least a forty-foot-high bank barn, the kind with oaken first floors above livestock penning and feeding areas below. The cavernous hayloft was empty and showed no evidence of having sheltered fodder for years. Three or four window hatches hung akimbo by only one hinge, and while the tin roof seemed porous, the roofline and superstructure of the barn were straight and sturdy. The vertical support columns and horizontal crossbeams were of the peg-and-hole connector types, and they were all of hand-hewn 8" X 8" dimensions, the hewing scars quite evident. Patches of faded red paint were still visible here and there, but for the most part the old edifice was now of exposed siding, probably of poplar wood that weathers rustically and is coveted by builders to add character and charm to new and remodeled houses and offices. On a thick rope strung over and through a large pulley, a hayfork dangled from an extended, roofed overhang. In its time used to hoist hay bales up to a loft opening, where they were pulled in by sinewy arms and steel hooks, it now suggested a kind of inquisitional or puritanical device used to exact wails and confessions from sinners. A grass and gravel covered bank, supported by crumbling concrete walls, ascended to wide middle doors leading to an alleyway that ran between about ten horse stalls. Above the doors, various livestock skulls were affixed, including a horned Hereford, a longhorn steer, and a tusked boar that seemed to glare in unison down upon those who would dare trespass on this ominous property. On the right side of the barn at ground level, an open door revealed an equipment room housing numerous cycles, machetes, and scythes that swung on chains and ropes from beams.

Stepping around the side of the barn, we opened the latch of a sagging gate and passed through what had once served as a cow pen, in which an old pump and trough had in earlier times watered cattle but now served only as symbols of bygone days. Once into the fields of the twenty-two acre tract, we gained a better perspective of this gothic spectacle.   To hundreds of vertical posts with branchlike appendages were tied thousands of multicolored jars, bottles, and jugs that made the tabletop terrain tantamount to some kind of extraterrestrial cropland. As if the skulls above the barn doors were not deterrent enough, a multitude of cattle, sheep, and goat skulls were impaled on pike-like poles and served as sentinels watching for interlopers. The wind, however, was the catalyst of horror, shaking and rattling the glass containers in a way that made these eerie figures animate in a phantasmal tableau.   The clinking glass cut through the air like an aural knife, and the frequent gusts over the openings of the containers were facsimiles of thousands of human mouths blowing over the tops of pop and beer bottles. Had it not been for the presence of my big brother, who I was sure could lick any man alive, the howling bottles would have frozen me in terror.

Added to this bizarre scene were other ghostly phenomena situated strategically among the bottle figures. About eight or ten life-sized Indian figures on horseback, cut from tin and painted in black, were nailed to 4 X 4 posts in silhouette fashion; blowing in the wind, they flapped back and forth, creating gutteral sounds that might have been interpreted as, "Leave this place! Leave this place!" Several rough-cut-wood frames held old iron church bells with tin strips attached to their clappers, and they emitted other-worldly sounds that amalgamated with those from nearby fixtures to create a spine-chilling, raucous concert.

I asked my brother, "Have you ever seen anything like this before?"

"Matty, I've never even read of anything like this before. We've seen it and know it exists, but now let's get the heck outta here!"

Retreating toward the barn and lane again, we could see my brother's date now outside the car, waving frantically and motioning us to hurry. We raced through the bottles and past the fence gate to the car, where she was pointing and stage whispering, "There, there between the house and the chicken coop!"

We turned and saw a tall but hunchbacked man with a ragged black beard and mustache wearing a long black coat and a crumpled black derby. He was moving toward us slowly but resolutely while mumbling and gesticulating at the sky. We scrambled into the car and backed out of the lane quickly. Once on the county road, we noticed that the sky had darkened more, and streaks of lightning were now bolting between black clouds. Was the specter-like man trying to warn us of an impending storm and danger or calling down the wrath of God? Was he the eccentric and mysterious owner or simply a drifter whose refuge we had invaded? We would likely never know.

Ten years later, I was in the second semester of my freshman year at Aquinas College, and, along with the standard core coursework of Mathematics 102, French 102, Logic 101, and Theology 120, I was enrolled in Composition 102. Having already written 300 to 500-word narrative, expository, and argumentative essays, my last assignment of the semester, due in mid May, was a descriptive essay. Sr. Ludmilla Dandridge, Ph.D., was most explicit in her oral and written explanation of the assignment. The essay could describe anyone, anything, anyplace, or any phenomenon, but it must reflect a careful rendering of an element of the real world. Emphasized in the written directions was the need to incorporate image-evoking descriptors but to avoid any embellishments or fabrications. The purpose of the assignment, as she had discussed in class, was to improve students' observations and sharpen their skills in capturing and rendering details.

Casting about for someone or something interesting enough to describe, I squandered in frustration and vacillation five or six of the ten days allotted to write the paper. To date, I had received a C+, a B, and a B- on my previous three papers, and my hopes for a B for the course lay with the final essay. I rather acutely needed to nail an A to insure the course grade I sought to bolster my cumulative grade-point average. Strangely, the idea of describing the Bottle Farm took a day or two to crystallize among my cluttered and racing thoughts.

Unlike the light bulb that appears above the heads of inspired cartoon characters, my recall of the Bottle Farm returned to me only by degrees. Once I rolled the paper into my typewriter, however, the details came back to me in a steady flow. I decided to re-create the road trip taken with my brother, and I pretty much retraced our visit to the Bottle Farm detail-by-detail. Drawing frequently upon my handy thesaurus, I picked the most graphic adjectives and adverbs I could apply to my haunting experience. The more I wrote, the more I was convinced that this essay would be the *piece de resistance* or the signature work of my Nobel Prize for literature. It would likely be selected for a national periodical, never mind the Aquinas literary magazine, *The Exponent.* (Other disciplinary majors on campus called it *The Spot,* as they considered that moniker commensurate with the size of an English major's brain.)

Once the draft was completed, I continued to tinker with the text to refine the descriptors and phraseology to a degree that would make Sr. Ludmilla's eyes glaze over in awestruck delight. Would she read the paper aloud in class, as she had done with some written by two or three of the Comp 102 superstars? Would she ask for a meeting in her office to discuss possible publication of the piece? Or would she place it on reserve in the Aquinas library to be read on-site by those seeking exemplary prose? The possibilities were myriad and endless.

On its due date, I proudly deposited my paper with the others on Ludmilla's desk, feeling sympathy for the creatively challenged souls whose work would pale conspicuously with my bottle-farm masterpiece. With only three class days remaining in the semester, Monday and Wednesday were spent in discussion of two or three of the readings in the rhetoric, as participation in all of the semester's discussions was ostensibly taken into account in determining final grades. On Friday, the last day of the class, Ludmilla took only a few minutes discussing issues related to the papers before returning them graded and dismissing her students early.

Turning back the cover page, I found a D+ sneering at me with the cruel disdain of an arch villain toward a noble hero whose grip is faltering on the side of a cliff before he plunges to his death on the awaiting rocks. Under the recorded grade were the dreaded words: "See me."

I, of course, went directly to Sr. Ludmilla's office, where she seemed to have anticipated my arrival. When I inquired as to the basis for such an abysmal grade on the paper, she replied, "Mr. O'Flynn, you were told quite explicitly that your descriptive paper could relate to any actual person or thing, but you not only chose to fabricate this nonsensical bottle farm, but you incorporated phenomena and descriptions that far exceed even the limits of verisimilitude for a fictional story."

"Sister, with all due respect, everything I described actually exists or at least did exist years ago. I may have been a little too graphic in describing some of the items on the farm, but I didn't fabricate anything."

"Take care, Mr. O'Flynn; don't add false statements to your situation."

After several efforts to describe the location of the bottle farm as best my memory served, she allowed that she would change my grade to a C-, but she maintained that if such a place actually existed, she would surely have heard of it, as Aquinas College was relatively close to Southern Ohio.

When my grade report arrived in the mail in the second week of June, my Comp 102 grade was, as expected, a C+, and it did nothing to move the GPA needle north. I do not know whether my disappointment was greater in regard to my final grade in composition or that my veracity had been so summarily impugned.

Some weeks ago, my brother and I were reminiscing about some of the notable adventures of our youth that were mostly experienced separately, owing to the difference in our ages. One of the very few we had together, as both he and my other older brother had regarded me as an albatross or a Typhoid Mary, was our trip to the Bottle Farm. Notwithstanding his being the driver and prime mover in our trip, my brother could remember few of the roads we had actually taken to the farm or exactly where it was.

"I certainly remember going there and what a weird place it was, but it was so long ago, I probably couldn't drive right to it again, even if it still existed. Ya think it still does?"

"Ya know, that's a good question. Did I ever tell you I wrote a paper about it when I was in college?"

"How'd ya do on it?"

"Terrible! The instructor thought I was makin' it up, and she gave me a crummy grade because the assignment was to describe someone or something that actually existed."

"It did. Didn't ya tell'er?"

"Yeah, but it didn't do any good. She pretty much accused me a lyin'. I still think about that miserable grade occasionally."

"Well, it probably makes up for all the times ya got a better grade than ya deserved."

"Yeah, right! Anyone who'd see my college grades would know two things."

"What?"

"One, I never cheated, and, two, I never got a better grade than I deserved."

The next day, I decided that I would do some research to see if there was any documentation or any recorded discussion of the Bottle Farm. I searched the Internet, and rather easily and to my total surprise, I found an entry with a great deal of information.

The Bottle Farm was the brainchild and creation of one Winter Zellar "Zero" Swartzel, a direct descendent of the original settlers of Jackson Township, Ohio. He was a natural born showman, teacher, and eccentric and quite possibly the grandfather of American Pop Culture. He lived from 1876 to 1953, and, distaining the labors of the agrarian life followed by his brothers, he and a friend embarked upon a bicycle trip to New York, and then turned around and headed west across America. Following that, Swartzel traveled the world and collected a wide variety of items with which he would later fill his home.

Chiding Americans for their wanton wastefulness, "Zero" Swartzel began to use his farm property for a massive collection of thousands of items, particularly the beverage containers cast aside by profligate Americans. His farm near Farmersville, Ohio became a field of glassware of all kinds that he mixed with bells, sculptures, bed frames, silhouettes, and other "art" discarded by wasteful humans. He named his most elaborate and most salient work in bottles "Kindly Light" and "Full Measure."

The farm provided fascinating listening experiences for neighbors from the bells and glass twinkling in the wind. Residents of nearby Farmersville, Ohio could hear the lyrics and melody of "The Old Rugged Cross" drift across the farm-land when loudspeakers projected the song on Sunday mornings. The bells on grazing sheep added to the mystical effect. The Bottle Farm attracted visitors from every state in the nation, save Delaware. Dying in 1953, Swartzel bequeathed the farm to the community to create the Farmersville-Jackson Township Joint Recreation Park for the enjoyment of children. Now razed to the ground, the house and outbuildings are gone, as well as all the strange collections of the Bottle Farm. In their place are a swimming pool, baseball diamond, tennis courts, picnic grounds, and walking trails.

If only the Internet had been in existence when I was in college, I could have printed the information about the Bottle Farm and handed Sr. Ludmilla the ocular proof. "If," as the saying goes, "a bullfrog had wings, he wouldn't bump his ass every time he hopped." Under any circumstances, finding the information about the Bottle Farm was a marvelous revelation and genuine enjoyment for me. Just having such an experience with a sibling that over many years became more and more exalted and cherished in my mind made me want to thank old "Zero" Swartzel. Like the children to whom he left his farm for their enjoyment, he had, without ever knowing so, provided me with a magical and memorable experience that far exceeded the lingering thrills and emotions of any amusement park, ocean beach, dude ranch, or commercially hyped venue. In my mind at least, the Bottle Farm was my brother's and mine; I knew of no one else who had even heard of it (other than Sister Ludmilla, of course), never mind visited or experienced it. As long as my memory will serve me, I can travel there on that windswept and dank March day and feel the nearly tactile ambiance of the Bottle Farm.

Of all the information gleaned from the Internet, however, one piece was more absorbing for me than the rest. Mentioned almost perfunctorily was a reference to a peculiar caretaker who looked after the Bottle Farm in "Zero" Swartzel's absence. He was described as being a scruffy and bearded hunchback, often wearing a long black coat and tattered black derby. He was known to walk into Farmersville each week for groceries and other supplies. He spoke to no one he passed, and the dogs in the area would typically become agitated, howling and barking.

Inspired by the information, especially about the caretaker, I decided to call my brother who, I knew, would treasure this noteworthy information.

Ringing his cell phone, I could hardly wait to tell him the news.

"Hello."

"Hey, do you know who that old guy was who came at us in the driveway of the Bottle Farm that day?"

"No! And I don't give a damn! It's two o'clock in the morning, you jackass!"

The Yearbook

> *Sweet are the uses of adversity,*
> *Which like the toad, ugly and venomous,*
> *Wears yet a precious jewel in his head;*
> *And this our life, exempt from public haunt,*
> *Finds tongues in trees, books in running brooks,*
> *Sermons in stones, and good in every thing.*

—As You Like It
William Shakespeare

Evan Garvey withdrew the dusty yearbook from a jam-packed bookcase that dominated the man cave of an elegant home, in which he resided after incremental increases in the value and quality of several houses he had occupied over many years. This *Ramrod* edition chronicled the last year of his fourteen years as an English teacher at David Copperfield High School. Wiping the red and white cover, he carried the annual publication with him over to the leather chair behind his large desk, plopped down, and propped his feet on one of the lower drawers.

Garvey had now been retired for ten years from a thirty-year career in secondary education, divided between fifteen years in the classroom and fifteen years in administration. Examining the *Ramrod*, he reflected upon his experiences that ranged from some of the most onerous and precarious situations to one of the most prestigious and enviable positions in Ohio. For the last twelve years of his career, he had been the principal of Maplemont High School. The Maplemont community was characterized by its opulent and massive homes and populated by its urbane and affluent professionals whose offspring were typically high-achieving scholars bound for colleges and universities classified as "most competitive" by guidebooks and profilers. A mixture of hard work, taxing assignments, and dumb luck had secured his position at Maplemont High School, but many a day in his career had taken him home crestfallen and discouraged. Maplemont parents, unlike those in numerous communities, were engaged in and supportive of their schools. While they rarely, if ever, defeated a school levy and wholeheartedly applauded and appreciated good teaching, they were most demanding and discerning in regard to school personnel and programs.

Perusing pages of the yearbook, Garvey contrasted the dynamics of working in a school like David Copperfield with that of Maplemont. He had functioned in two other high schools between his employment at Copperfield and Maplemont: one year as the high school English Department chair in the upper middle-class community of Sparta and three years as the high school principal in the rustically impoverished community of Carmel. While every assignment and venue effectuated satisfying and gratifying situations, each also delivered career questioning circumstances, fears, and developments.

After fourteen years of teaching English at Copperfield High School, Evan's head had been turned by the offer to serve as English Department Chair at the upscale Sparta High School. The assignment was most attractive: only four teaching periods with two regular English Literature classes and two Advanced Placement English Literature classes. The remaining three periods of the school day were for observing and supervising the other eleven members of the department. The only hitch that he did not anticipate was that one of the members of the department had been passed over for the position, and she zealously believed and discordantly maintained that she should have been selected. Evan spent the entire year defending himself against the boorish machinations and verbal attacks of the disgruntled teacher. When his doctoral advisor at the university urged him to gain some administrative experience at tiny Carmel High School in an Appalachian region of Ohio, he made the jump eagerly into the perils of a principalship.

Carmel was a high school of approximately 300 students who were typical of the children of low-income and poverty-line parents. The teachers and support staff were obscenely underpaid and some performed at a commensurate level. An alarming number of students, as a local minister had told Evan during an office visit, were the victims of incest and other abuse, but while most parents were poorly educated and culturally ignorant, they were hard working and well intentioned. A district that had not passed a school levy in thirty years remained in abysmal achievement because "that schoolhouse was good enough for me when I was a kid, and it's good enough for them kids now." Evan's venture into school administration was a baptism of fire that included a rapid-paced indoctrination into local parlance and behaviors and not-so-veiled physical threats. Irate Carmel parents who called him would sometimes cut to the chase with overtures like "I'm gonna kick your ass!" which would differ from angry calls he would receive in later years at Maplemont that were more judicious: "I'm going to sue your ass!"

Garvey closed the yearbook, tilted back the swivel desk chair, and contemplated the various schools where he had worked and the positions he had held, some clearly more lucrative and prestigious than others. He believed, however, that for nearly every educator that first teaching experience was the most memorable and meaningful; it certainly was for him.

When Evan Garvey stood for the first time before his freshmen English classes, David Copperfield High School served the quiet bedroom community of Highgate, which was densely populated at the time by highly educated and professionally successful Jewish parents, who lived in the most well-appointed homes in the district and who prized skilled educators among the most meaningful influences in their children's lives. Highgate was also a concentration of middle-income, white Anglo-Saxon Protestants, who lived in two sprawling plats of brick, ranch homes. Additionally, in the township that fed students into Copperfield High School, a substantial population of low-income white families lived in post-Korean War houses, built as starter homes for armed forces veterans. Those veterans had largely departed, and their prefabricated boxes were now in severe disrepair and occupied by impoverished families of Appalachian origins. The Highgate School District was, therefore, about 99% white.

Over the first five years of Evan's teaching at Copperfield, his classes began to reflect a growing number of black families that had moved into the district, but the student population remained preponderantly white. When, however, two federal housing projects were installed within the district, the black population of students soared in the schools seemingly overnight. The enmity that was nearly indigenous among the black students in the projects and the white students in the decaying houses boiled over quickly, and soon the fights that began on the morning buses spilled into the parking lot, hallways, and classrooms at Copperfield High School. Tensions had reached critical mass one afternoon in early September when the principal, Patrick Adams, announced over the public address system at about 1:30: "Teachers, go to your classroom doors and lock them, and let no one in or out." Adams' announcement was too little too late, as a huge number of white and black students had already exited the building and gathered on the knoll by the boulevard, taunting each other, while an enormous black woman was turning 360 degrees and threatening everyone with a .357-magnum hand gun. The conflict resulted in the arrival of multiple units of local, sheriff, and state patrol cruisers and officers; closed the schools for the remainder of the week; and put the community under martial law for six days. Teachers and administrators spent the week in meetings and sensitivity sessions, and black leaders in the area addressed the staffs in each building. David Copperfield High School was now in dramatic transition. White families commenced an exodus that began slowly but increased in volume over the succeeding years.

Evan James Garvey was an Irish Catholic who had been reared in an all-white neighborhood and educated in a Catholic and nearly all-white grade school, high school, and college. As such, he had been taught in environments of strict discipline and unqualified deference to and respect for teachers. His early days as an English teacher in a public high school revealed that his experience base would rarely serve him in his teacher-student relationships.

Among his first-week lessons in public-sector reality was that day when Evan and his good friend and fellow first-year teacher, Bill Burbage, were assigned to noon supervision in the hallway outside the cafeteria. The job assignment for the neophytes was to move lingering students out of the area and direct them toward their fifth period classrooms. When Evan had asked Burbage how he wanted to handle their year-long duty, his more savvy colleague, who had been educated entirely in public schools, said, "I'm gonna sit on that heat radiator over there and try to keep the crease in my pants."

Evan was planning to take his responsibilities much more seriously. So, when Louie Hendricks, the 6'5" power forward on the basketball team, was hanging around the cafeteria doorway that day, programming one of the cheerleaders, Evan approached him and said, "I'm sorry, but you'll have to move along toward your classroom." Looking down at Evan over his trendy Benjamin Franklin sunglasses, Louie warned, "I go where I want and do what I want." Evan walked over to Burbage, who asked, "What's up?" Evan replied, "I'm gonna sit here with you and try to keep the crease in my pants."

Garvey looked at the image of the ram mascot of Copperfield High School, rendered in *bas-relief* on the cover of the *Ramrod.* The Rams were quite competitive in nearly all sports, but after about four years of Evan's teaching at Copperfield, the athletics director asked him if he would add the coaching duties of a tennis program that had heretofore won only six matches in its history. When Evan said, "I play a lot of tennis, but I've never coached it," the A.D. replied, "That's all right; we really just need some supervision and someone to drive the van. No one expects you to win."

Evan took up the gauntlet and announced his first practice in the second week of March on the school tennis courts that were surfaced in blacktop and equipped with nets made of chain-link fencing. Those who reported for practice were among the most pitiable looking specimens he had ever seen on any kind of field or court, and few actually owned a tennis racket. In fact, some were from the post-Korean War development out in the township, for whom previous tennis coaching would have been as likely as winning the Irish Sweepstakes. Evan used the time to demonstrate the grips for the backhand and forehand, while reviewing the scoring and rules. After running some laps around the five courts, the group was dismissed for the day. The next morning before first period, Evan went to the Physical Education Office and talked to Lissa Poole, one of the P.E. teachers, and asked her if she had any extra tennis rackets she could let his players use.

"All I have that I can spare are some old steel rackets with wire strings that are basically indestructible. They're in the storage room."

"I'll take all you've got."

Returning from the storage room, she handed Evan nine racquets that seemed to predate Bill Tilden's Wimbledon Championship days.

"I'll get them back to you as soon as I can."

Lissa smiled condescendingly and chortled, "No hurry."

Throughout that first season, Evan spent most of the practice sessions instructing basic tennis technique, etiquette, and strategy. As the season proceeded, some players lost interest and quit, some managed to obtain more up-to-date racquets, and some developed a little skill in groundstrokes, volleying, and serving. Evan started a player ladder that consumed much practice time for challenge matches that were more fun and competitive for players than the interscholastic matches that were virtually all 0-5 blowouts. The last match of the season, however, was against the rather economically depressed Denton High School, the doormat in nearly all sports in the ten-team league. Although the match came down to a marathon, three-set exchange of unforced errors, the second doubles pulled out the third set 7-5 to give the Rams a 3-2 victory and a season ending record of 1-17.

The next September, Evan decided to attend the open-gym sessions for basketball players, hoping to upgrade the tennis team with more athleticism. Since open gym was, by Ohio High School Athletic Association guidelines, just that, he could as a non-basketball coach jump into the full-court games and make some inroads with the kids. His strategy paid off, as two freshmen fraternal twins, who would by their senior year reach 6'6" and 6'7" in height, told him they would be out for tennis after basketball season in the spring. One was an adequate athlete, the other a splendid multi-sport talent.

Over the next four years, more athletes gravitated to tennis, and eight to ten developing players formed the nucleus of a rapidly improving program that now included a very competitive varsity and reserve team, the A.D. having hired Evan an assistant coach. Evan spent his own money renting late-hour time in the winter at the local indoor-tennis barn that provided his players a greatly reduced rate for court use. He and the athletics director painted the school courts, replaced the metal nets with soft-cloth nets, and built a rebound backboard against the fence for kids to work out on their own. By the second year, the team was 7-11; the third, 11-7; the fourth, 15-3; and the fifth, 17-1. What was especially meaningful in the fourth and fifth years was winning the championship of a league that included Maplemont High School. Maplemont had won its league championship prior to that for over thirty years in a row. Little did Evan know at the time that he would one day be the principal of Maplemont High School.

He had stepped down after his fifth year of coaching to write his master's thesis, but as Garvey ran his hand over the ram head on the cover of the *Ramrod*, he realized that he never felt more alive than during those years with the Copperfield tennis team.

Paging rapidly again through the *Ramrod*, Garvey reached the group picture of the drama club, and it reminded him of his only attempt at play direction. By the school year of the yearbook he held, he was, of course, in his last at Copperfield, and his semester-long Shakespeare class, which was supposed to be limited to 25 students, had through the guidance counselors' cajoling him now reached 36.

Evan had had the Shakespeare course foisted upon him a few years before by the department chairwoman who had taught the class for years and, through tedious line-by-line explication of the plays, reduced student sign-ups to about five or six. In an effort to bring Shakespeare alive even more, Evan decided that last year to divide his class into two groups of eighteen, and assign one group to the production of a scene from *The Merchant of Venice* and the other group a scene from *A Midsummer Night's Dream*. He committed the four weeks prior to the Christmas break for the project, and then he used two days per week for class study and turned students loose for the other three days in the classroom or the Dickens Theatre for scene development. Evan knew nothing about blocking or staging, so he gave limited directions and advice. With some reservations about how well

these juniors and seniors would handle character assignments, set design, and Elizabethan costuming, he basically
let them fly on their own.

Evan's plan was to schedule the performances during the
noon hours for the Thursday and Friday before the
Christmas break and to invite his other students to attend of
their own volition. As word spread among the English teachers and other staff, he was petitioned for access to the performances for other classes. The idea "grow'd" like Topsy.
Although he feared a colossal flop, the performances went on
to a packed Dickens Theatre each day. His students did not
disappoint. Using a dual-purpose backdrop designed and
painted by the students and wearing costumes created by
and sewed by them, both groups relied on a non-character
narrator to set the scene and establish the storyline for the
audience. While his Shakespeare students were dazzling
other classes and staff members, Evan was busting his buttons in the back of the Dickens Theatre.

Tucked in the back of the *Ramrod*, Garvey found a 5 X 7
group picture of himself with the casts of *A Midsummer
Night's Dream* and *The Merchant of Venice*, and he ached to
see and talk to those kids again.

Garvey moved to the back pages of the *Ramrod* and found
the individual, formal pictures of the seniors; among them
were the last he had taught at Copperfield. When he reached
the F's, he found the picture of Jasmine French, who was
integral to the most bittersweet experience of his career.

By Evan's fourteenth year at Copperfield, he had grown
considerably in his ability to work effectively with the minority students whose population was growing in direct propor-
tion to white flight from the district. He had in truth become
something of a favorite among black students, largely
because he had learned to avoid taking himself too seriously
while maintaining a firm control of his classes after some
easy exchanges and spontaneous humor with the kids in the
hallways and as they drifted into his room. He knew he was

often the butt of their esoteric humor, but he gave them no indication that he heard the chortles, if not knowing their basis. More often than not, he figured they had to do with something physical, especially among the girls.

As a white teacher, Evan had learned the hard way that with black students he had to give them the space to accept what he wanted for them educationally. Part of that process was developing an understanding of their tolerance for any white teacher's efforts, which did not include a fatuous attempt to act black. Even he knew that to black students nothing was more ludicrous, if not insulting, than a white male who had spent his entire life in a Caucasian culture trying to be hip to the nuances of their dialogue. Evan had watched with embarrassment one of the middle-aged assistant principals trying to assume a black persona as he greeted and interacted with minority students.

One indicator of Evan's growing acceptance was reflected in the recently adopted teacher advisory program, a homeroom replacement period in which students stated their preference for a specific TAP teacher as they scheduled classes for the next year. Intended to allow for informal counseling sessions while announcements and other homeroom activities were conducted, the TAP classes pretty much evolved into twenty-minute gab sessions that had lost the elements of counseling but had gained advantages in socialization among white and black students. By its third year, the TAP sign-up was showing a preponderance of black students who were seeking Evan as the teacher. Technically limited to twenty students per section, Evan was being besieged by counselors to take four or five more junior or senior students who were pushing them to be included.

One of Evan's particular favorites, who was in her third year in his TAP class by his last year at Copperfield, was Jasmine French; an outspoken, studious, and beautiful black senior girl who was every inch of six feet, although claiming to be 5'11". She was blessed with the most flawlessly smooth skin he had ever seen on a human being. As a straight-A student with close friends among the academic elite as well as on the periphery of serious delinquency, Jasmine was both book and street smart. For Evan, she could be his greatest advocate or his most irritating critic. He had had her as one of his students in his semester-long advanced composition and Shakespeare classes when she was a junior, and, as such, she was now the resident expert on all of Evan's strengths, weaknesses, and idiosyncrasies. She was not loath to expound publicly upon any.

As a member of the National Honor Society, Jasmine had provided a stirring speech at the induction ceremony that spring, touching deftly, with related examples, upon the themes of character, leadership, scholarship, and service. With her hair exquisitely coiffed and dressed as she was in a sleeveless black dress accented by a string of pearls, she possessed the regal look of an African princess. She spoke with an eloquence that night that approached the verbal mastery of an Oxford don, but when the need arose or the mood served, she could dress, act, and talk like a street walker. She could do or be anything she wanted.

As the driving force that year, Jasmine rallied support to have Evan read the names of the graduating seniors at commencement, an honor not taken lightly by any faculty member because it represented real and long-term acceptance among the students. When Evan received the news from Patrick Adams, he accepted the offer with outward appreciation and humility, but he was also doing a bit of a mental victory dance.

At commencement, Evan was in his best dramatic form reading the graduates' names and any of their attendant honors or scholarships. He was almost halfway through the nearly 450 graduates when his oratorical ship hit the iceberg. Well into the glow of his theatrical reading of the names, he failed to notice that when he reached the last student's name in the left-hand column of a two-column-per-page format, he had turned to the next page in his copy of the program, skipping the right-hand column of the previous page entirely.

With all the graduates assembled behind Evan as he faced the huge audience in the arena, students were to file out of their rows of seats and approach biology teacher Mike Sendig off to his right to receive their diplomas before crossing in front of Evan to receive either a rose or a ribbon from counselor Christine Barhorst on his left.

The trouble began when Evan read the first name on the next page after skipping about thirty students. Noticing that no one had crossed in front of him, he looked at Sendig, who just shook his head at Evan while holding the student in place whose name had not been announced.

Evan's swagger and confidence level dropped like a rock, but he tried the next name with no luck. Sendig continued to shake his head, and a hush fell over the cavernous facility. Because of the huge size of the senior class, Evan simply could not know every student, and he could not see anyone he recognized stacked up behind Sendig. He read the next name; Sendig shook his head. Perspiration was beginning to roll over Evans ribs like the Niagara River over the Falls.

Like the babbling fool he had become in a matter of moments, he dropped back and punted, imitating the faceless voice on television when the transmission breaks down, "One moment, please."

Evan was a helpless child in a "fair field full of folk,"* and in spite of his request for a time-out, he was no less clueless after the thirty-second pause, which seemed like an hour, than he was before. He plowed ahead with the next name.

Hearing her name read, a student about two rows behind those ahead of her, stood up, walked around everyone, and approached Sendig for her diploma; raising a murmur that rolled over the audience like a wave at a football game. At this point, Demetrius Jackson, senior class president, came to Evan's rescue and, looking at the befuddled teacher's page placement, reoriented him to the right spot.

Once things got moving again, an unmistakable voice about four or five rows behind Evan said in a volume loud enough for him and others around her to hear but not the audience, "I knew we shouldn't have asked that honkey to read our names!" Students within earshot broke into unsuppressed laughter. The speaker, of course, was Jasmine French.

After the ceremony, Evan wanted to get to his car as quickly as possible, but he was surrounded in the lobby by students and parents who were not only forgiving but who were doing their best to laugh him out of his mortification.

On Monday morning, on the counter below his mailbox stood and old trophy with masking tape over the original inscription, bearing the words: "Silver Tongued Teacher Award." Leaning on it was a note, which said: "To Mr. Garvey: We still love you! The seniors." The handwriting looked a lot like Jasmine's.

Garvey walked the yearbook over to the bookcase and pushed it horizontally on top of a shelf full of books. He wondered whether he had accepted the job as the English Department chair at Sparta because of its prestige or because of the lingering mortification from his Copperfield blunder. Maybe it was both. The year at Sparta as department chair and the three years at Carmel as principal merged with his Copperfield experience to prepare him for the pressures at Maplemont as principal. Many factors contributed to Garvey's very satisfying years at Maplemont, but since failures tend to teach more than successes, perhaps the result of the borderline hubris he brought to that Copperfield graduation taught him to avoid the hauteur wrought by overconfidence and self-satisfaction.

* *Piers Plowman*—William Langland

A Highland Halloween

What seemed particularly odd [...]
Was that though these folks
Were evidently amusing themselves,
Yet they maintained the gravest faces [....]

—*Rip Van Winkle*
Washington Irving

Finishing my most recent short story one late Halloween afternoon on my Highland County horse farm, I saddled my spirited but gentle mare, Sally, fully expecting a languorous ride into the twilight. Sally, a striking fifteen-hand sorrel, is one of three Quarter Horse mares on the farm, two of which belong to me, and the third I board for a neighboring high school student for whom I occasionally serve as a writing tutor.

Neither Sally nor my other mare, Sadie, had been ridden in over a week, and the aromatic and unseasonably warm autumn air beckoned us to the riding trail. Once brushed, saddled, and bridled, Sally allowed me the barest time to find both stirrups before she pranced from the barn, through the barnyard, and down the hill next to the paddock toward the creek. I gave Sally her head, and she cantered along the trail between the front bean field on the left and the wooded creek line on the right. The October colors were in grand profusion, and the wind jitterbugged through the trees, making the leaves a kaleidoscope of sundry designs and dazzling hues. I had been so busy with my fiction writing and barn renovations throughout the fall that I had not appreciated the magnificent foliage now gracing the rolling topography of the land. Astride a thousand pounds of horseflesh, however, I found my senses awakening to the tactile stimuli beneath and around me. Rather than take the loop to the left and head in a general direction back toward the barnyard, I extended the ride significantly by taking a more circuitous route across the wondering spring-fed stream.

Crossing the sandy creek bed, Sally lunged up the craggy bank and into the fallow field above, and then we headed toward the remnants of the old "house in the holler" that once served as temporary living quarters for itinerant field workers when the farm was vastly larger than its current ninety acres and sustained all manner of grains and live-stock.

"C'mon, Sally, let's circle the old house on the buggy lane."

The buggy lane was actually a nineteenth-century county road used by family doctors, traveling salesmen, and casual visitors to reach remote farmhouses and residents, but it had long ago been integrated into the present farmstead. We loped across the former tobacco field and entered the buggy lane that was now just a tractor run taking us up the steep hill and opening into a five-acre hay field that provided a panoramic and vibrant view of the farm.

"I wish we could freeze this vision and moment, Sally girl! Take a mental picture with me before we head back to the barn."

Sally nickered in what seemed to be an affirmation of her mutual appreciation of the scene before we descended the hill on our roundabout return trip. We picked up the pace a bit because I hoped to avoid total darkness during the some-what perilous rutting season, and we were soon heading up the quarter-mile gravel lane toward the house and barn. Before ending this serene and almost surreal horseback ride, I decided to pull Sally off the lane and direct her along a branch of the bridle trail that wound through a dense wood-lot, which simply begged to be traveled, notwithstanding the imminent darkness. What may have unconsciously prompted my deviation was the faint but now growing aroma of burning leaves and logs. As we started up the hill, Sally shied twice before I began to hear what she had obviously detected. At her first reluctance, I had thought she smelled or heard the presence of deer, which would invariably cause her anxiety, but I soon began to hear the faintest sounds of human voices somewhere beyond our vision among the trees. Rounding a bend in the woods, I could see in the dusk a group of four figures seated on logs and stumps in a rough circle around a campfire, and the sight augured for me a gathering of goblins on this Halloween night.

"Easy, Sally girl, easy," I half-whispered to my equine pal, trying more to assure myself than my mount.

I approached the figures apprehensively and halted Sally about twenty feet from their seated location. As the dancing flames erratically illuminated these figures, I beheld four of the most curiously attired men I had ever seen. Not one deigned to acknowledge me; so casting caution aside, I stepped down from Sally and walked toward them in a most deferential manner, though I was vexed by the gall of these intrusive masqueraders.

"Good evening, gentlemen. Might I inquire as to what you're doing in these woods and why you're keeping a campfire at this time on my property?"

They continued to murmur among themselves, ignoring me as if I were no more than a hoot owl on a sycamore branch down in the marshes.

"Excuse me, gentlemen. I don't mean to appear inhospitable, but I'd like to know what you're doing here on Halloween night in my woods. If you need assistance, I'll gladly help, but as the proprietor of this farm I believe I'm owed an explanation of your intentions."

After a disconcerting delay, a gangling, sunken-faced, and long-nosed fellow rose from his stump-seat and addressed me rather disdainfully. He was about 6'3" but seemed to weigh no more than 170 pounds. He was attired in a white shirt and neckerchief, black waistcoat and jacket, black pants and colonial boots, and a velvet three-cocked hat.

"My good man, you are in the company of four renowned travelers whose stories are the stuff of legend. We are en route to Oxford, Mississippi, where we intend to enroll at Ole Miss University under the provisions there for designated citizens, and we'll then collaborate on the great American novel. We sojourn in this sylvan setting tonight to plan the balance of our itinerary and to begin preliminary discussions of what will be our timeless tome."

"Tell 'im, Ichabod," said a raspy voice behind the billowing pipe smoke below the standing figure.

To say the temerity and attire of this indignant fellow took me aback fails to render my amazement. Said I, while gathering my composure, "You're not Ichabod Crane of Sleepy Hollow fame are you?"

"He is, young fellow, and it might behoove you to hear our stories and learn the reason for our journey together," interjected the white-bearded kibitzer who then resumed puffing on his Little Ladle tavern pipe.

This odd-looking smoker wore a black Puritan hat, a bright blue coat with cuffed sleeves, yellow knickers, white knee-length stockings, and brown high-topped shoes with buckles.

The imperious splinter of a man resumed, seemingly annoyed by his companion's interruption.

"You've apparently heard of me, Mister..."

"Shannon, Mike Shannon," I said quickly. "I...I own this place."

"Yes...yes, you told us that. Since you know something of me, Mr. Shannon, I hasten to tell you that theories of my demise at the hands of the headless Hessian are very much in error. True, that Philistine Abraham 'Brom Bones' Van Brunt did pursue me as I made my way from the Van Tassel farm on the rambunctious Gunpowder that storied night, but the pumpkin he hurled from his steed sailed over my head and struck a nearby tree. Having lost out to 'Bones' in my pursuit of the hand and wealth of the beautiful Katrina Van Tassel, I quit Sleepy Hollow as a schoolmaster immediately and returned covertly in the night to my roots on the Hudson Eastern Shore. Since then I have earned my bread as an itinerant teacher, and taking my philosophy of 'Spare the rod and spoil the child' with me, I have often applied the ferule I now hold to the backsides of reluctant scholars. I have lived off the largesse of small country villages until the residents figured out...er, decided that my pedagogy was not the equal of my sustenance. I have, however, made the close acquaintance of many a comely maiden during my travels."

"So, you really are Ichabod Crane!"

"That's right Mr. Shannon, and perhaps you've heard of me," said the puffer.

"Everyone's heard a you Rip," said a third figure seated on a log with his left leg extended to the right of the smoker. He was a youthful specimen in a dark-blue, single-breasted frock coat that bore several brass buttons down its front and was girded by a wide leather belt clasped by an equally wide brass buckle with a *bas-relief* U.S. on it. His sky-blue trousers were tucked into mid-calf, black infantry boots; and his long, flaxen hair was swept back under a rumpled, navy-blue kepi cap with the insignia of two crossed rifles on the front and top.

"I daresay that you know a bit of my story as well," continued the resolute old gent, as he tapped the embers from the clay pipe on his knee and then loaded two more logs on to the flickering fire. He stood for the first time and stepped closer to the blaze, rubbing his hands in a warming action.

"I'm a British-American villager of Dutch descent and a rather skilled raconteur, if I do say so myself. Quite likely, you've heard that Rip Van Winkle was a man who loathed profitable labor, but I submit to you that the pensive, indolent man who'll take a drop now and then is much more of a social asset than the man who's in perpetual pursuit of filthy lucre."

"Well," I started to say, "I have read that..."

"Please don't interrupt my apologia, young man. Where are your manners?"

"Uh...sorry!"

At this point, he withdrew from his inner coat pocket a pewter flask and quaffed a healthy slug of its contents. Wiping his lips on his sleeve, he continued.

"You probably heard that while fleeing a termagant wife one fall Saturday afternoon, I and my faithful coon dog, Wolf, hiked into the Catskills, seeking relief from her relentless carping. Happening upon some diminutive fellows who were playing at ninepins, I joined them for some comradeship and grog. I believe they may have been some of Henry Hudson's crew, but that's another story. Of course, I'm sure you know that I fell asleep from the effects of their brew and slept for twenty years. And it was a peaceful slumber at that. Now, I want you to know that because a man eschews the back-breaking labor of the noble husbandman and prefers the company of his doting hound to his pitiless spouse does not mean he is remiss as a citizen. I often regaled the youngsters of the village with my fanciful tales, and I was always at the ready to help any neighbor with his farm work, especially if he happened to keep a flagon of rum on the premises. Those of my predispositions are the dessert of society not its castor oil."

He sat back down and took another pull on his flask before scooping some tobacco from his pocket and into the bowl of his pipe. With his rekindled pleasure in hand, he winked at Ichabod, who nodded in obvious approval of his companion's account.

"Well," I said, "you have both removed any misunderstandings regarding your lives and experiences, but..."

"Ya ain't hered all our steries yet, mister!" interjected the figure seated to the right of the young man in blue. He was most unkempt, and he reeked of stale whiskey even in the fragrant woods. He wore a filthy slouch hat over long, twisted black hair, and his buttonless coat hung open, revealing a pair of ragged overalls and a grimy shirt that looked on-loan from Ezekiel, son of Buzi. His long, salt-and-pepper beard provided all the creature comforts sought by judicious cooties.

"Now hold on, Pap," said blue boy. "You'll get your turn, but I'd like to know if this gentleman has heard of me."

"And you are..."

"Henry. Henry Fleming," said the earnest young man as he stood and placed a bandanna on the stump-seat behind him.

"Fleming...Henry Fleming. Let me think," I said.

"Does the Civil War help you any?"

"Are you..."

"Yes, I am. And no doubt you probably hold me in very low regard. As a callow eighteen-year-old, I volunteered for the 304th New York during the Civil War. I was filled with a sense of patriotism and glory, and I, of course, couldn't wait to see some of that celebrated action. Naturally, prior to the first engagement, I began to see the very real and imminent danger of battle. As you probably know, I ran from the fight in my craven fear and met retreating and advancing columns as I did. Having engaged a fellow Union soldier aggressively, he struck me with the barrel of his rifle, leaving a bloody gash on the side of my head. As you also probably know, I returned to my battalion, and when my head injury was mistaken for a battle wound, I acquitted myself well from that time on."

"Yes, Henry, we discussed your case each year in my American literature classes when I was teaching high school English. *The Red Badge of Courage* was part of the juniors' required reading."

"Well, quite likely, I was often found derelict in my behavior by your students for running from my first battle, but those young people should know that when the fanfare and falderal that sends us off to war is behind us, we front-line fodder are left with the realization that what lies before us is a bit more meaningful than the 'mom-and-apple-pie' reasons for the grisly slaughter. When boys and men lie on blood-soaked fields watching entrails spill from their bellies, they're no longer fighting for the honor of their mothers; they're bawling for the comfort of their mothers."

A hush fell over the encampment, and no one seemed to know when or how to commence conversation. I broke the silence with an affirmation of Henry's insights.

"Actually, Henry, our discussions of your reaction were often lively but equally divided. Naturally, the more macho and naïve students were critical of your initial behavior, but even they decided that you redeemed yourself at length for the most part. Others felt like you did what came naturally to an inexperienced youth facing the realities of war. They often said..."

"Lissen 'ere," said a voice from under a dirty slouch hat. "Ya wanna hear suthin' wirth talkin' 'bout, lissen a my stery."

The man in the filthy hat with a lid that flopped open bent down between his knees and brought up a half-gallon, stoneware whiskey jug and took a long pull on its contents. As he bent down again to replace the jug, the lid of his hat flopped open again. He then rose to a precarious semi-upright position to hold court.

"Lotsa folks think I'm sumkinda snake inna grass cuz ol' man Twain made me a shamelis thief, a chile abuser, a drunkin' sot, 'n a hateful bigot. Well, mebbe I am, but all I'z iver wanted wuz ta git my rights. Folks git down on me cuz I uze that N-word now 'n then 'n cuss better'n ol' Sowberry Hagan. Well, I ain't Pap Finn hisself if I don't pervide a pow-erful suhvice ta th' govment."

"Actually, Mr. Finn," I said to this offensive lout, "you made every attempt to steal young Huck's reward money, and your ill-treatment of him is well-documented. Your attitude toward the black professor was the essence of racial prejudice."

"Now, ya looky 'ere. That p'fessor thought I wuz jist white trash 'n..."

"That's your opinion, but..."

"Now, hol' on a minute and don't innerrupt. My pint is that Twain feller used me as a lowdown shiflis skunk ta show 'is readers th' ugliness of th' prejudice tha' galls you so. He made me an example awat not ta be. That sneaky scundrl had all th' ugliness of bigotry comin' outta my pie hole. So, I'm jinin' these fellers ta make my case 'n hep 'em set record straight in th' book we're writin'."

About that time, Pap started listing to the right, so Henry Fleming guided the eloquent self-defender to his seat where he resumed a mouth-to-mouth love affair with his jug.

"It seems, gentlemen," I began, "that I have fallen upon a troupe of transients who have captured my fancy. You see, I'm a bit of a journeyman writer myself, and a retired teacher, Mr. Crane. With your permission, I'd be delighted, honored in fact, to accompany all of you to Mississippi and hear more of your stories along the way. I couldn't tarry long in Oxford, of course, but I would certainly take two or three weeks away from the farm to enrich my literary insights and gain immeasurable grist for my own stories."

They said nothing at first, but then they all leaned in toward the fire and began a muffled confab. In the meantime, Sally, whom I had nearly forgotten, was waiting in abeyance. She actually began nudging me with her nose in a not-so-subtle reminder that she wanted to return to the barn and be divest of the saddle. At length, however, Ichabod turned toward me and seemed to speak for the group.

"Mr. Shannon, if we were to take you with us, you'd need to understand that we'll be traveling clandestinely and often under cover of darkness."

"Oh yes. I certainly understand your need to remain under the radar."

"Under the…radar?"

"Under cover; that is, unseen or undetected."

"Yes, yes. But how would you manage your affairs, your farm while you were away?"

"I tutor a neighbor boy and board his horse, and he'd be delighted to earn some spending money and keep his horse here cost-free for the month of November by looking after the horses and tending to the house and barn."

Ichabod leaned in to the huddle again and whispered some comments. At length, he stood once more and said, "Mr. Shannon, we have decided to take you along. Since you have an affinity for writing, we would ask that you chronicle our trip and note the desirable or beneficial traits in us that may not have emerged in our oft-studied stories."

"I'll be ready in the morning. Will you be staying here in the woods tonight?"

"Indeed, we will, but mind you, we'll be leaving before dawn. You'll need to join us no later than 5:00 a.m. You'll also need a knapsack with your provisions for the journey."

"No problem. I have everything I need for backpacking."

"Backpacking?"

"Traveling by foot."

"We shall expect you before daybreak, Mr. Shannon. Be sure to bring pencil and tablet."

"I will, and good-night!"

"Good-night, Mr. Shannon!" the group said in chorus.

I swung a leg over Sally, and we picked our way back to the barn. I turned her out quickly and hurried to the house, where I called Cameron and told him what I needed over the next three weeks or so. Then I packed clothes, provisions, and materials into my backpack and began planning the fascinating travel journal I would compile with these escapees from the pages of classics. By the time I crawled into bed, I heard one o'clock strike on the grandfather clock down in the foyer. I probably did not fall asleep until after two.

When I opened my eyes again, the daylight was breaking through my bedroom window. My alarm clock, set for 4:30, had not gone off. It was now 7:25. In my excitement, I had not pulled the pin to activate the alarm mode before I had fallen asleep. I threw on my clothes and grabbed my backpack and a Gatorade. I raced back to the woods, frantic that I had held up the group. When I reached the familiar spot where they had camped the night before, they were not only gone, but not one sign of a campfire could I find.

"That's weird," I said aloud. "I can understand that they left without me, but how did they dispose of all remnants of the fire?"

As I began a closer inspection, I discovered that also missing were the stumps and logs that my mysterious friends had sat upon, and there were no footprints or any signs of a recent gathering. Suddenly, the cold realization befell me that I had either been hallucinating or dreaming.

"You fool," I said to myself, "what would make you think you were actually going to take a walking trip to Mississippi with four fictional characters?"

I sat down on a large rock and began to laugh at my own foolishness. After much reflection and rationalization, I concluded that the apple cider I had been drinking to slake a thirst during my previous day's writing session must have been laced with brandy or rum.

"Yes, that was it. Old man Jessup must have slammed some hooch into that batch, and I was three-sheets-to-the-wind without knowing it."

I rose to pick up my backpack and return to the farmhouse. Taking a final look about me, I noticed something peculiar at the base of a large, nearby poplar tree. There, lying together, I found a Little Ladle pipe, a ferule, a half-gallon stoneware jug, and a bloodied bandanna. I froze.

Fourth Period

Nature [...] likes that we should be her fools and playmates.
Direct strokes she never gives us power to make;
All our blows glance, our hits are accidents.
Our relations to each other are oblique and casual.

—Experience
Ralph Waldo Emerson

Standing before his fourth period students at Thomas Jefferson High School for the first time on that early September morning, Kevin Kielty was not sure whether he would survive the next fifty-four class minutes, never mind the next 179 class days. He had taught just three classes so far in a career that had only begun three hours before at 8:00 a.m. He wondered whether this foundation English class would be punishment for exaggerating his foreign language mastery in order to be hired for a teaching assignment that included two French I classes in addition to the three English I classes he was actually qualified to teach. He had told the assistant superintendent, Karl Ladd, who interviewed and hired him, that even though he lacked foreign language certification, his twelve semester hours of undergraduate course work had made him entirely capable of teaching two freshman French classes. Fortunately, Ladd knew hardly a word of French because the most cursory sampling of Kielty's skills would have exposed the applicant as a pretender. Since Kielty's interview had taken place in late August, Ladd had asked for a certification waiver from the State Department of Education for the French component of the assignment in order to fill the position quickly. Little did he know that Kielty would only manage to stay about one chapter ahead of his French students.

With the bell now having rung, the reason why only fourteen students were assigned to this section began to crystallize for Kielty all too quickly. The class, the composition of which was thirteen boys and one girl, was a surly-looking group of toughs whose ages ranged from 14 to 16. Kielty might have felt sorry for a lone girl in the company of thirteen rough-edged boys, but she looked like she could whip all but two or three of them. Trying to avoid the appearance of the neophyte that he was, he began with a roll call that had calmed his nerves a bit in the previous classes.

"Ceifert Blevins."

"Here. I like Ceif better."

"Okay, Ceif."

"Marvin Butler."

"Here. Marv."

"Got it. James Raymond Cass."

No response.

"James Raymond Cass."

No response.

A scattering of sniggers and guffaws swept over the room.

"Is there no James Raymond Cass here?"

Finally, an obviously older and more physically mature student, said, "Jim-Ray Cass's here, and that'd be me."

"Okay, Jim-Ray it is."

"Bradley Combs."

"Here. Make it Brad."

"Clyde Durban."

"Here."

"Woodrow Gullet."

"Woody."

"Mitchell Helton."

"Here. Mitch."

"Henry Humerick."

No response.

"Henry Humerick."

No response.

Woody Gullet slapped a somnolent, corpulent boy on the back of the head.

"Henry Humerick."

"Oh, here. Sorry!"

"Gerald Medford."

"Here. Call me Gerry."

"Travis Pickleseimer."

"Here."

"Jason Reffits."

"Here."

"Constance Rench."

"Call me Connie."

"Thornton Tillman."

"Thorny."

At this point, a row began in the back of the room between Connie Rench and a sandy-haired boy who looked like he could have been Connie's little brother. Kielty stopped the roll call to settle the disturbance.

"Hey, what's goin' on back there?"

"You tell 'im ta quit callin' me a slut. You say that again ya little shit'n I'll wup your ass for ya."

"Oh yeah!" came the bravado response from a puny but pugnacious kid who appeared only half-sure she could not.

"What's your name?" asked Kielty.

"Randy Vance," said the runt and put his head down on his desk.

"Better shut yer yap, Vance," warned Jim-Ray over his shoulder. "I've seen her whip guys a lot bigger'n you."

Jim-Ray was at least sixteen and easily six-feet tall. An Elvis Presley look-a-like, with The King's same smoldering countenance and sonorous voice, Jim-Ray's jet-black hair hung in his eyes in front and duck-tailed in the back. His demeanor boded a volatility that enhanced his good looks but belied what Kielty would eventually learn was his inner goodness and good will. He was dressed on this warm September morning in what would be his uniform throughout the school year: Levi jeans, motorcycle boots, and a white T-shirt under a black leather jacket with a Bardahl Oil patch stitched to the back.

With Randall Vance identified, Kielty had finished the roll call.

He began activities by printing his name on the chalkboard and then pronouncing it. Following that, he distributed copies of the grammar textbook and then the anthology that was geared for the most fundamental, high school reading level.

"Please print your name on the next available name line inside the back cover of both books."

"Are we gonna read everything in this book?"

The question came from a curly-haired blond boy who held up the anthology and who looked as if he had slept in his shirt and pants.

"I'm sorry. What's your name?"

"I just told ya, Gerry Medford."

"Well, Gerry, two things. First, raise your hand if you have a question. And second, probably not all but most of it."

The groans that met Kielty's response might have suggested the likelihood of a forty-lash flogging for each student before the end of the school year.

Kielty spent the remainder of the class period reviewing what the students would be doing throughout the year and offering his enthusiastic overtures regarding the long-term value of their English I studies. The students, of course, spent the remainder of the class period needling each other and paying Kielty the most minimal attention.

That night, Kielty prepared carefully for his French I classes, thinking they would be his most immediate and difficult challenge. He was wrong.

While his French I classes and two of his three English I

classes were time-consuming in terms of preparation, the dynamics of his fourth period English I class were a baptism of fire for this callow novice. Nothing seemed to be working although he had begun the year with the anthology, selecting stories he thought would be of interest to his reluctant readers: "The Interlopers," "The Monkey's Paw," "Wine on the Desert," "Leiningen Versus the Ants," "To Build a Fire," and others with adventure-type storylines. He learned rather early, however, that not only were his students reluctant readers, they were profoundly provincial.

Kielty gained considerable insight into the geographical limitations of his students in early October when he had them taking turns reading orally from a simplified and abridged edition of Carl Stephenson's "Leiningen Versus the Ants." Surmising that his students were unfamiliar with the story's setting, he interrupted the reading to ask the class where the rainforests were. In response to what he thought would be easy pickings for as least some of his students, he received only thunderous silence.

"C'mon, somebody knows where the rainforests are."

At length, a very tentative and chubby hand rose from the back of the room. It belonged to Henry Humerick, the short, portly boy who was easily the kindest and most cooperative student in this class of recalcitrant "scholars."

"Yes, Henry. Where are the rainforests?"

"Well...I ain't sure, Mr. Kielty, but I think they're past Cincinnati."

Several heads nodded vigorously, offering Henry reassuring affirmation.

What could Kielty say? Henry was right. Thomas Jefferson High School was in Southwest Ohio, and the rainforests were sure as hell past nearby Cincinnati.

Through the fall, Kielty's classroom management skills evolved from a naïve expectation of his own experiences in parochial-school discipline and behavior to a more relaxed understanding that he had to roll with the punches a bit. He tried to mix each class session with grammar and literature and other language arts exercises, but in his way of thinking, he was not turning the corner in his efforts to win the enthusiasm of his fourth period students.

Over his lunch in the lounge on a Thursday in mid October, he vented a bit in regard to his frustrations with his fourth period students, citing their seeming disdain toward any of the anthology selections he had offered as bait to awaken their reading interests. Few in the lounge at the time were sympathetic, as all were seasoned teachers who had paid their dues with foundation classes that were typically assigned to the "newbies" who deserved all the grief they got. Seeming to gain no one's real attention, never mind anyone's sympathy, Kielty shut up and finished the now-cold and always rubbery hamburger and French fries he had brought from the cafeteria.

At length, the very sophisticated, svelte, and stylish Jean Miller lowered her newspaper and said, "Why don't you try something that speaks to them?"

Jean Miller was a married woman in her mid-thirties who was pretty much the queen of the English Department; not to be confused with the chairperson of the English Department. The chair was almost by definition a matronly, stoic, and shorthaired woman or a stodgy, balding, and pot-bellied man. Always dressed to the nines, Jean had the face, figure, and features that turned male heads of every age all over the building. Owing to her stature, Kielty had lacked the chutzpah to broach any conversation with her.

"I'm not sure what that would be," said Kielty, knowing that staff royalty had just deigned to address him.

In a surprisingly indulgent manner and with a disarming familiarity with his given name, Jean Miller finished her thought. "Kevin, I'm just finishing a unit on the novel with my foundation juniors, and we've been using a newly released book by S. E. Hinton, *The Outsiders*. I have a class set of paperbacks that we'll no longer need after tomorrow, and you'd be welcome to use it with your freshmen. It'd probably be just as suitable for them as it was for my juniors."

"Well, actually, Mrs. Miller, I'd take your advice on anything, but what's it about?"

"It's about teenagers who're socially and economically divided, but Hinton's realistic dialogue and character development carry the storyline very effectively. *The Outsiders* is really new, so very few of our students have heard of it, let alone read it. Why don't you stop by my room after school today, and I'll give you a copy to read over the weekend."

That afternoon Kielty went to Miller's room and discovered that the woman whose persona suggested aloofness was actually very warm and engaging. Yes, she knocked his eyes out, but she also offered him the first real encouragement that he actually had a future as a high school English teacher.

"Kevin, you have to give yourself a little time. There's no one here who didn't struggle at first. Most of us inherited the tough classes as beginners, but I still ask for at least one class of foundation juniors just to keep my management skills sharp. Besides, I've reached the point where I believe it's much more important for me to like the kids than it is for them to like me." She smiled and winked at him impishly, but before she sent him on his way, she added quite seriously, "Don't hesitate to stop by here to talk whenever you'd like to unload a bit."

Over the weekend, Kielty poured through the book, and by Sunday night he had decided to begin the second quarter with a study of the novel, specifically, *The Outsiders*.

He borrowed sixteen copies from Jean Miller (at least two students would lose theirs), and in the first week of November, he had his students reading orally in class and a few pages silently at home.

Miller was certainly on-the-mark in her assessment of what his fourth period kids would enjoy. In fact, hands went up immediately at the beginning of each class to read aloud. Naturally, some struggled mightily with the oral reading, and once, Thorny Tillman offered his critique of Ceif Blevins's very halting efforts.

"Damn, Blevins, let somebody else read. You're screwin' up the whole story!"

"Up yours, Tillman!"

Kielty jumped in. "Okay. Okay. You're doin' fine Ceif. Just finish the paragraph."

Thanksgiving break arrived, and Kielty used the days to prepare a few chapters ahead in the French I text and plan some reader-based writing assignments for his two other English I classes. By late November, his fourth period students were closing in on the conclusion of *The Outsiders* when the bottom fell out of Kielty's nascent confidence as a teacher. Interrupting the oral reading periodically for discussion and interpretation, Kielty made the mistake of referencing one of the characters as a "punk," a term he used casually in conversation and believed was pretty innocuous. From the back of the room, he was put on notice. Jim-Ray Cass had taken exception to the term and offered his editorial comment.

"That ain't no way ta talk about anybody!"

Stunned, Kielty could only say, "What?"

"You'd be lookin' for trouble in my neighborhood if you called somebody a 'punk.' You shouldn't be talkin' that way."

Violating the cardinal rule of avoiding a war of wills with a student in class, Kielty got his back up and dressed Jim-Ray down in front of the others. With his macho on the line in the presence of his buddies, Jim-Ray would not recant and left Kielty with no alternative but to send the student with a disciplinary referral to the assistant principal, Dorothy Thombs. Thombs was a shrewd and strong educational leader who was at the vanguard of area women working in secondary school administration.

Basically forgetting his own note to Thombs, Kielty was

summoned during his plan period that afternoon to her office where he found Jim-Ray already talking to the assistant principal. After admonishing the student in Kielty's presence for his behavior, Thombs told him to assume the position; whereupon she withdrew a paddle from her closet and delivered two stunning whacks across his buttocks that her forceful forearm could easily deliver. Serving as the lawful witness to the corporal punishment, Kielty was awed by Thombs' deliberate approach to institutional justice and Jim-Ray's stoic response to the blinding pain. After the whacks, which Kielty surmised the student had experienced before, Jim-Ray turned to the young teacher and muttered, "Sorry, Mr. Kielty!"

Having walked Jim-Ray to the door with her hand on his shoulder and in whispered conversation, Thombs returned to the astonished and regretful Kielty.

"You were right to refer Jim-Ray, Kevin. He needs someone to rein him in at times, but please know that his father is an abusive drunkard, and on any given morning, Jim-Ray may have to step over his dad on his way out the door."

Kielty, of course, felt awful. He knew that he was as much at fault for the incident as Jim-Ray, but another kid from a hardscrabble environment had paid the price.

By the end of the first week of December, Kielty's fourth period students had finished their study of *The Outsiders*, but their enthusiasm for reading and discussion had crashed and burned. Clearly, the other students were aware of what had likely taken place in Thombs' office, and Jim-Ray's subdued demeanor had told the tale. Kielty, in spite of his efforts to make a grammar unit tolerable and paragraph writing easy, was convinced that he had completely backslid to where he started with these students in September. When he tried to make small talk with any of them before or after class, he received only the most mechanical responses.

In the second week of December, he decided to take Jean Miller up on her offer to drop by and talk, so he popped his head into her doorway on Thursday afternoon before heading home. She was seated at her desk grading some papers.

"Jean, you have a minute?"

"Hey, Kevin, what's up?"

"Pardon my French, but I kind of shit in my own nest with one of my fourth period students, and I think it's had a pretty demoralizing effect on the whole group."

He explained to Miller what had developed with Jim-Ray, and even though she listened intently, he was pretty sure she had heard most of it already. What he thought she did not know was that he believed he was just as much at fault in the incident as Jim-Ray.

"Have you told him?"

"No. I'm not sure how I'd approach him."

"Since fourth period's the last before lunch, just mention to him that you'd like to talk to him for a minute after class and before he heads for the cafeteria. That way, everyone else will have cleared out quickly, and you can have some private time to share your feelings."

"He'll just blow me off, I'll bet."

"Maybe not. Give him a chance."

"Thanks, Jean! I'll try it."

As he started to leave, Jean said, "Hey, you wanna have a Christmas drink with some of us next Friday after school?"

"You mean with some of your staff friends?"

"Yeah. We don't bite."

"Well, I just meant that I wouldn't wanna barge in on your party."

"Nonsense. We'll all be at the Boar's Den around four o'clock for a few hours before we head out for Christmas. We'll be glad ta have ya. You do take a drop, don't ya?"

"Yeah, I drink. Thanks!"

The next day, Friday, Kielty hailed Jim-Ray and asked him to stop by his desk after class like Miller had suggested. Jim-Ray agreed, but he obviously suspected some further trouble.

After class, Jim-Ray played it cool and let the others file out first so no one would see him stop at Kielty's desk.

"Jim-Ray, I...don't really know how to start this, but I just wanted to tell you how sorry I am about what happened in class and then in Mrs. Thombs' office. I know I was as much, if not more, to blame as you were. When I watched you take those whacks because of me, I felt like a criminal. I still don't condone your response to me in class, but I understand it. I'm learning more about teaching in this class than you guys are about English. I'm sorry I used a term that was offensive to you. All I ask is that in the future if I say or do something in class that offends you, just give me a chance privately to make amends. That's all I wanna say."

Jim-Ray did not respond to Kielty immediately. He just stood looking down at his boots. He walked to the doorway to leave, but stopped, turned around, and said, "You're not a criminal, Mr. Kielty."

The next week was the last before Christmas break, and as is typical in most high schools, the students were easily distracted and difficult to manage. Kielty's fourth period students were very much the norm, but for him the atmosphere made his relationship with his foundation kids a little easier. Just before the bell ended fourth period on Friday, Kielty took time to wish them all a merry Christmas and a happy New Year. When the bell rang, however, they did not bolt for the door; they all shuffled up to Kielty's desk. Connie Rench did the talking.

"Mr. Kielty, we know you think we don't like you, but you've got it all wrong. We just don't like English. But you make it as much fun as you can. We really like you a lot."

Woody Gullet broke in, "Tell 'im about the present, Connie."

"I'm gettin' there! So, we got you a little present to let you know how much we like ya. Where is it?"

"Here."

Travis Pickleseimer handed her the gaudiest wrapped

present Kielty had ever seen. Connie handed it to Kielty. No one moved or said a word.

Opening the box carefully, Kielty found a dozen mono-grammed hankerchiefs with the stitched initials of his full name: Kevin John Kielty. Kielty was so close to tears, he nearly lost it.

"Thank you, guys!"

They filed out, shouting almost in chorus, "Merry Christmas, Mr. Kielty!"

That afternoon, Kielty joined some of the fun-loving veterans at the Boar's Den. He bought Jean Miller a Dewars Scotch Whiskey and said, "Today, I received from my fourth period students one of the nicest gifts I've ever been given. Last week, I received from a good friend some of the best advice I've ever been given. Merry Christmas, Jean Miller!"

"Merry Christmas, Kevin!"

The Tackle

Upon these fields of friendly strife
Are sown the seeds
That, upon other fields, on other days
Will bear the fruits of victory.

—West Point Gymnasium
General Douglas MacArthur

They marched into the stadium in total silence and formed themselves in rectangular companies over the lush grass and soft dirt of Yankee Stadium on this most unseasonably warm October Saturday. The Corps of Cadets had made the 50-mile trip from West Point that morning to the Big Apple to support the Army football team in its staggering assignment to defeat the heavily favored Duke Blue Devils, who were ranked fifth in the United States by most of the media and spoiling for a blowout victory to advance themselves toward a national championship. A sparse crowd of about 25,000 dappled a stadium that could accommodate more than 60,000. Few New Yorkers had expected anything less than a gridiron massacre that would leave the Black Knights strewn like piles of shredded armor and chain mail over a glorified salvage yard. The venue of Yankee Stadium had been chosen five years before when Army was a national power itself, and a home game at cozy Michie Stadium high above the Hudson would not have accommodated the enormous demand for tickets.

As the cadets moved toward their midfield seats on that Indian summer day, they maintained a somber bearing that suggested decorum suited more for an inaugural parade than for a football game. When the last cadet double-timed into the stands, however, the others erupted into non-stop chants and cheers that would, over the course of four grueling quarters, have an attritional effect on the Blue Devils' resolve.   As traditional, the cadets remained standing in what was expected of the Corps, no matter the actual score or the anticipated score.

When the teams returned to the field from their dressing rooms after a previous warm-up, the Duke fans in attendance gave their team the kind of confident cheers that all but said, "Let's kick their butts and get the hell back to Durham!" The Corps of Cadets, however, had another kind of game in mind, and they bolstered their team with a nearly relentless "Go! Go! Go!" which suggested a squad that was itself nationally ranked rather than one mired in mediocrity and rebuilding from humiliating losses that had the Army brass grinding its teeth and screaming for improvement. The consecutive losses to Navy were embarrassment enough, never mind the blowouts sustained against the likes of Pitt, Southern Cal, Northwestern, and Georgia Tech. A cheating scandal had decimated the Army football talent, and Coach Ed Bracken had been left with only a handful of recruited players and a number of intramural midgets to begin the rebuilding process.

In the spring semester some years before, scores of cadets, many of whom were football players, had violated the West Point Honor Code in regard to a difficult exam taken by the junior class. The succinct code, which said, "Cadets do not lie, cheat, or steal, or tolerate those who do." absolutely forbade any student discussion of the content of exams, tests, or quizzes in-progress. Living in close quarters and following the same curriculum, young men in their late teens and early twenties faced almost impossible standards of deportment. In the case of the cribbing scandal, however, there was no confirmed exchange of specific answers, but some cadets told others who had not yet taken the exam to study certain chapters or pages. Those who knew of the exchange of information but remained silent rather than report violators to the honor committee were judged as guilty as those who had given or taken advice. When news of the disgrace broke, it became the lead story in virtually every daily and weekly broadsheet in America. Nearly all of the guilty cadets who stood before the honor committee were subsequently dismissed from the Academy by a student tribunal that was likely more reproachful than any faculty council might have been. The following years found the recruiting of football players especially difficult, as many "blue chippers" feared that the demands of the West Point academe and code would be their undoing. The irony of the event was that on just about any other campus in the country, the advice would have been considered common courtesy, and the silence would have been regarded as reasonable expectation. To this day the dismissed cadets and their punishments remain controversial and debated.

Duke stormed into the game on October 27th with a perfect 6-0 record that included convincing victories over South Carolina, Wake Forest, Tennessee, and Purdue. Army sauntered into the game with a much improved record of 4-1-1 that boasted one meaningful win over a very respectable Michigan team at Ann Arbor but also a head-shaking loss to Northwestern in Evanston and a frustrating "down south" 0-0 tie with Tulane that saw two Army touchdowns nullified. Three All-American candidates led the Blue Devils: ferocious tackle Ed Mershad, versatile quarterback Worth Leamon, and lightening halfback "Red" Staley. The Duke down linemen averaged over 250 pounds, and their running backs and ends were nearly all over 200 pounds. The Duke linebackers and secondary were fast and versatile, and they filled holes and hit receivers quickly and violently. Army was fielding a cadre of promising but green athletes who were beginning to play well above their experience levels, but the typical Army back was about 190 pounds, and the bigger Army linemen went about 220 to 225.

As the home team, Army took the field in their very traditional black jerseys with gold and gray trim, gold pants with black stripes, and time-honored gold helmets that gleamed in the sunlight from an indigo sky. Duke spread over the field in their all-white pants and jerseys and their blue helmets with white stripes.

Duke had won the coin toss and wanted to make a defensive statement early by sending Army to a demoralizing three-and-out possession, so the Blue Devil captains chose to kick-off in the first half and then to receive at the start of the second. As the Duke kicker was placing the ball to his liking on the tee at the Blue Devil 40-yard line, Cadet yearling, or sophomore, defensive back Jack Hadley was standing nervously on the Army 5-yard line while the frenzied cheering of nearly 2,400 cadets rang in his helmet. Hadley, who would not turn 19 until October 31st, was fast and lean at 6' and 185 pounds, but looking downfield at the behemoths who were likely to book him a suite at Walter Reed that afternoon, he was fidgeting with his jersey sleeves and adjusting his chinstrap in an anxiety equaling what he would feel on a future day just prior to a helicopter assault landing in the Mekong Delta.

As the Duke kicker approached the ball, the rowdy cadets began the "ooo-wha" that marked the opening kickoff of every Army game. The kick was magnificent, sailing high and deep and giving advantageous hang-time for the Duke defenders who were flying down the field. Hadley took about three steps forward as the ball settled into his arms at the 7-yard line. He took only four or five steps to his right before one Duke tackler flew by him on his left. Spotting a gang of white jerseys lunging towards him on the right, Hadley reversed his direction and headed toward the visitors' side of the stadium. Again, juking two or three tacklers, he turned up field, as many Duke players did the same. Approaching the 45-yard line, he appeared to be running out of room when two tacklers angled in on him near the sideline. From nowhere came Army end Nash Chambers with a devastating block that took out both Duke players cleanly. After that, it was just a footrace between Hadley and Duke's safety valve who had slowed a bit when the Army ball carrier seemed bottled up at the 45. Jack Hadley raced into the end zone and into Army football history.

The Rabble was going crazy in the West Point cheering section. The Blue Devils were jawing among themselves, and the Duke faithful were stunned and silent. Even the Duke cheerleaders seemed in a trance on the sidelines, gazing blankly at the Yankee Stadium scoreboard after Army kicker Rox Carpenter stuck the extra point attempt straight through the uprights. The score was now Army 7 and Duke 0, with only 15 seconds gone from the first quarter of play.

"Go! Go! Go!" The cadets had resumed their chant.

Carpenter unloaded a superb kick-off to the Duke 2-yard line, but the return man pin-balled out to the Blue Devils' 18. Worth Leamon went quickly to work under-center, and he deftly faked and boot-legged time and again, either riding the ball into big, fast backs or rolling out to complete short but efficient passes that tormented the pursuing defense. From the Army 30-yard line, Leamon rode Duke's 222-pound fullback Cotton Cash into the line of scrimmage behind a huge Blue Devil line before withdrawing the ball and heading around end past a double-teamed Lowell Shane for sixteen yards to the Army 14-yard line. The Army defense was sucking wind when manna from Heaven fell upon Yankee Stadium in the form of Duke's sensational halfback "Red" Staley's fumble on the 12-yard line. Army linebacker Leroy Lundstrom fell on the ball and delayed the inevitable for a stoked-up Duke eleven.

Army quarterback Pete Borland, calling his own plays, remained conservative deep in Army territory and handed off twice to left halfback Pat Jarvis and once to right halfback Tommy Blanda. All three rushes went for short gains against an aggressive and stunting defense. Army's fullback, Freddie Ruschatz, punting from the Black Knights' 5-yard line, unloaded a towering spiral that sailed over the Duke punt returner's head and rolled all the way to the Blue Devils' 31-yard line.

For the remainder of the first quarter and for most of the second, the two teams exchanged possessions and protected field position, although with each exchange the Duke offense seemed to advance deeper and wear more visibly upon an Army defensive unit that was disadvantaged by a vast weight discrepancy and an oppressively hot day that had reached 85 degrees by the second quarter. Army's best offense was Ruschatz's punting, as he and Jarvis and Blanda were being straightened-up and pasted at the line of scrimmage, and Borland was running for his life trying to complete even short passes. The Army defense, led by senior end Bob Manus and sophomore linebacker Chester Roush, was distributing a few "snot-knockers" and "decleaters" of its own, as the linemen gang-tackled and swarmed to the ball, and the secondary of Hadley, Danny Zeigler, and Billy Wing were making the Duke receivers pay dearly for most every catch.

On the sidelines, head coach Ed Bracken and his offensive and defensive coordinators, Vince Lambert and Rollie Amen, were exhorting their players relentlessly and exacting every measure of effort from a game but overmatched squad. The excitable and animated Lambert would greet puffing players with what often sounded like "Yagn, yagn; yagn, yagn; yagn, yagn, yah!" The methodic and eloquent Bracken would calmly explain what to do and not to do, and the rigid and steely Amen would look dismissively at player cuts and bruises and exclaim," Play through it men, just play through it!"

With 4:42 left in the second quarter, Duke took over deep in its own territory after Ruschatz had angled a punt out-of-bounds on the 12-yard line. Leamon wasted no time. First he hit Cotton Cash over the middle with a pass that covered nine yards, and Cash did the rest, bowling over linebackers and defensive backs for a 27-yard gain on the play. On the next first-down, Leamon ran a sprint draw that slid the ball into Staley's hands, and then the fleet halfback blazed off-tackle for a fifteen-yard run that put the Blue Devils on the Army 40-yard line. Cash carried the load for the next three plays, and with 2:40 left on the clock, Duke was fourth-and-one on the Army 31. With the Army defense packed in to prevent the short blast for a first-down, Leamon rode Cash into the line before pulling the ball out and rolling to his left to hit 6'4", 228-pound Ronnie Miller streaking down the side-lines. Hadley flew over from his free safety spot, but at the 11-yard line Miller straight-armed the out-sized defensive back who hit the ground rolling, and the big, raw-boned end high-stepped into the end zone. Leamon, who was also the place kicker, calmly hit the extra point, and the splendid cadet effort in the first half was all but erased. Army took over on offense on its own 37-yard line after a nice kickoff return by Danny Zeigler, and then Borland hit one short pass to Donnie Steele and ran a keeper for six yards to run out the clock. The score was tied 7-7, but the Blue Devils had given notice to a benumbed and tired Army team that they could score and score quickly whenever they put their minds to it.

After the Army players grabbed some water and hit the restrooms, they took their seats on stools in the plush locker room where the likes of Mickey Mantle, Yogi Berra, and Whitey Ford had sat regularly during the months before. Bracken looked over a somber group that gave every impression that there was nothing left in the tank.

"You've just shown me more courage than I demand of any Army team, and there is rarely any limit to what I demand. You've demonstrated to the Corps that you deserve their unflagging support, and you've shocked a swaggering Blue Devil team that came in here today expecting a walkover. But you're tired now and you're hurting, and you've just seen a valiant first-half effort soured by a late

Duke touchdown. What did you expect? They're undefeated and ranked 5th in the country. Did you think they were going quietly into the night because you were leading 7-0? Did you think they were awestruck because you returned the opening kickoff for a touchdown? Did you think they'd fold their tents just because you laid a few good licks on them?"

Bracken paused, walked to one of the windows, and looked out for so long and in such a disconnected manner that he seemed to have forgotten where he was. When he turned and walked back again to speak, a raspy and emotional voice broke the quietude.

"Today, you not only have a chance to return Army football to prominence but to validate the very ethos of the Academy. You can show the nation, the world in fact, that it is possible to demand the highest ethical standards from young men in the classroom and still have them excel on the playing fields. You have within your grasp an epochal victory that will redirect Army football from the depths of ineptitude to the zenith of achievement. You can go down in history today, or you can listen to your fatigued and aching bodies and be satisfied with what you've done so far. You can be intimidated by a poised and celebrated opponent and surrender what could have been your legacy to West Point. I have no new strategy to impart at this time. I have no revised offense or defense. I have only the strength of character of this team that will take the field in the second half and give every measure of its will-to-win to send this Blue Devil bunch back to Durham with its first loss of the season. You can do it...you can do it...you can do it!"

Bracken turned and walked to the tunnel and waited for his assistants to review the first half and to plan for the second. When the team formed behind him in the tunnel to take the field again, Bracken felt an energy that he would later describe as almost ethereal.

When the Black Knights came out of the tunnel again, the Corps of Cadets gave them such a rousing cheer that it not only reinforced the renewed ardor imbued in the players by their coach, but as it resonated over the field, it created a curiosity mixed with an anxiety among the Duke team and fans who naturally assumed that the late first-half Blue Devil touchdown would have a devastating impact upon the spirit of the Army team and its rowdy cohorts.

Gathering starters on the sidelines, Army captain Al Farris addressed his teammates in a hurried huddle, and he offered his postscript to the Rabble's enthusiastic welcome and the coach's impassioned talk. "Ya know what we've got to do. We can't let 'em down. We can't let him down. They've brought us this far, now let's take 'em home!"

The second half, however, began much as the first had ended. Army kicked off to Duke, and the fleet return man Bobby Joe Cannon followed a massive wall of Blue Devil blockers and advanced the ball all the way to the Duke 47-yard line before kicker Rox Carpenter had to bring him down with a jersey tackle. Leamon went to work again methodically, mixing his plays smartly and catching the Army defense in all the wrong anticipations. Staley was his usual brilliant self, leaving Army defenders faked out of their jocks all over the field. On first-and-goal at the Army 3-yard line, Leamon faked to Staley, and then gave to Cash who blasted into the end zone, carrying two Army defenders with him. For the first time during the game, a momentary hush fell over the cadet cheering section, and Duke lined up quickly for the extra point. Manna fell once more upon Yankee Stadium. Leamon's holder bobbled the snap just long enough to give undersized but quick Army defensive tackle Braxton Chance the time to get his left hand on the kick and send it sailing low and wide-left.

"Go! Go! Go!" The cadets resumed their chant as if Army had just scored the touchdown. It was like the Deity had said, "Here's what I'm giving you today; the rest is up to you."

"Go! Go! Go!"

Even the Duke faithful seemed to sense something ominous about the blocked kick. Though their heavily favored Blue Devils had just steamrolled an Army defense, the Duke cheerleaders were now exhorting their team tenuously, not confidently.

For the remainder of the third quarter and the beginning of the fourth, the two teams played chess on a 100-yard board. The two field generals, Leamon and Borland, moved their troops strategically and safely. The heat and fatigue factors were, of course, taking their toll on both squads, but the out-sized Army linemen were suffering the most. Borland, however, was beginning to show the poise and skill that would soon establish him as one of the premier quarterbacks in the country. Mixing his ball-handling legerdemain with his pinpoint passing, he was starting to get enough time from a tiring Duke defense to move the Army offense with a confidence not heretofore exhibited. Blanda and Jarvis were beginning to make significant gains running wide and off-tackle, and the Black Knights were penetrating deeper into Duke territory with each possession. The undersized Army defense was also finding seams in the big Duke line, and it twice sacked a rather surprised Leamon and was holding Cash for short gains and forcing Staley wider and wider for minimal yardage.

With 8:57 left in the fourth quarter, the Duke punter sent the ball skillfully out-of-bounds on the Army 13-yard line in what was another strategic move to eat valuable time and preserve a precarious six-point lead.

When Borland came to the huddle, the rangy 6'2", 190-pounder looked into the sweaty and tired faces of his teammates. "We're not stoppin' this time. If you linemen can give us all you've got, Tommy, Pat, Freddie, and I are gonna give you six. Forty-six on two; forty-six on two."

Behind stellar blocking, Tommy Blanda carried two linebackers for seven yards. Rushatz and Jarvis did much the same as Blanda on the series, and the Army offense moved the chains incrementally down the field. Borland was brilliant, hitting most passes on the run, and once shoveling a left-handed exchange to Ruschatz just before being walloped by Mershad. With 4:02 left on the clock, Blanda took a pitch from Borland and dusted the outside linebacker and cornerback for a nineteen-yard scamper into the end zone.

Army 13 – Duke 13.

"Go! Go! Go!"

Rox Carpenter was unflappable, and he coolly gave Army a 14-13 lead.

"Go! Go! Go!"

Everything now seemed to be going right for the Army team, as even the Duke return man on the ensuing kickoff lost the ball in the late afternoon sunlight and had to fall on it at the 8-yard line. Leamon brought his troops onto the field with 3:41 left on the clock. It was an infinitesimally small amount of time when measured against the history of human endeavor, but it was a virtual millennium when given to the potent Duke offense with three time-outs at its dispose. On first-down Leamon dropped back to pass, but he pirouetted quickly in a planned quarterback keeper and headed straight back into what he figured would be a surprised Army line. The Black Knights stayed at home, however, and for the first time really laid the leather to the brilliant QB.

"Go! Go! Go!"

Duke returned to the line of scrimmage quickly, and on second-down, Cash got a tough two, but on third-down Staley was stopped in the backfield for a one-yard loss.

"Go! Go! Go!"

On fourth down, and with 2:48 left on the clock, Leamon called a time-out to plan what could be the last offensive play for Duke. When play resumed, the Blue Devils showed why they were the nation's #5-ranked team. Leamon took the snap and headed left in the backfield before handing the ball to the wingback who had peeled off and headed back to the right behind the pass-blocking linemen. Taking the ball from Leamon, he ran toward Staley, who had started around the right side but had pivoted and was now headed left. Staley took the ball from the wingback and then cut up field through a gapping hole created by the entire right side of the Army defense that had been fooled perfectly by the double-reverse. He was out to the Duke 40-yard line so fast there was nothing but green between him and the goal line.

This ghastly sight to the cadets in the stands and on the Army sidelines was like a Marciano punch to their collective solar plexus.

One black-jersey-clad defender, however, came out of the confusion, #87, defensive end Bob Manus. From his contain position he had shed his blocker and watched the ball exchanges that resembled a shell game. He was about ten yards behind Staley when the halfback hit the 30-yard line. Manus had some wheels, and Staley was not the same, rested rusher who had started the game. By the time he hit the 50, Staley felt like he was running a practice-field gasser, but he heard nothing but the frenzied cheering and saw nothing but the end zone. Manus had closed to within about three yards by the time the two had crossed the Army 40, but he was no longer gaining rapidly. It would have to be a desperation lunge to bring Staley down.

From the sidelines Bracken had been yelling, "Wait, wait!"

At the 20, Manus was within a yard of Staley but running out of room. At the 17-yard line, almost as if he could hear Bracken exclaim, "Now!" Manus leaped at Staley and hauled him down at the 7-yard line.

Duke fans were delirious. First-and-goal at the 7, and two time-outs remained for the Blue Devils with 2:30 left on the clock. In the West Point stands, exhilaration was tempered by grinding fear, but an Army team needed the Corps now more than ever.

"Go! Go! Go!"

Leamon wanted to score and leave nothing on the clock, so he took his time calling each play and bringing his team up to the line of scrimmage. On first-down, Cash gained three to the Army 4-yard line. On second-down, Army was waiting, and for the first time during the game slammed the tiring Cash backwards for a one-yard loss. Leamon called a timeout.

"Go! Go! Go!"

When play resumed, Leamon pitched to a streaking Staley who was dragged down at the half-yard line by Chester Roush.

With eleven seconds on the clock, Leamon called his last timeout, and the Duke manager threw the kicking tee onto the field for the obvious field goal attempt to win the game. In the huddle, however, Leamon rethought the field goal. They had already had an extra point blocked, and he would be asking his gassed linemen to hold a jacked-up Army defense out long enough to get the ball down and up cleanly. Anyway, the Blue Devils wanted a national championship, and beating an unranked, undersized Army team by only two points would not materialize that dream. To his tired but determined teammates, Leamon said in the huddle, "Let's go for it; it's just a damned half-yard!" Everyone nodded. Coming out of the huddle, Leamon threw the tee back to the sidelines.

With the offensive and defensive lines packed in tight, Leamon ran a quarterback sneak that created a black-and-gold and blue-and-white stack of flailing humanity. The referees called a time-out with one second on the clock to sort out the result. They found Leamon on the bottom of the pile with the ball pinioned beneath him about six inches short of the goal line. When the head referee signaled Army ball and pointed toward the Duke end zone, the cadets in the stands went wild. Hats flew; blouses waved; and voices went hoarse.

With one second on the clock, Borland took the snap on

the six-inch line, dropped back, and threw the ball out-of-bounds. The Rabble stormed the field and mobbed their exhausted team. The Duke players were gracious in bitter defeat, and they stayed on the field to congratulate Army players and cadet fans.

In a post-game interview, Worth Leamon said to a reporter, "I knew we were about to play a vastly underrated team today, but I didn't think we'd have to beat the entire Corps of Cadets!"

In his review of the game, Ed Bracken said, "Never has an Army team done so much for the image of the Academy. Never has an Army team shown such amazing resolve. Never has an Army team come so far, so magnificently. I shall never forget these young men!"

On the field that day were what would be in time five All-Americans, three Rhodes Scholars, numerous Vietnam War heroes, a few killed-in-action, many Ph.D.'s, and three lieutenant generals. The indefatigable spirit of one determined end would become integral grist for the orientation of plebes when they arrived each July to begin their transition to West Point life. But also, quite significantly, everyone in a blue-and-while or black-and-gold uniform provided testimony to what the game could still be today if played with mutual respect, by true students, and without commercial hype.

A Risk Well Taken

*Chuchundra, the muskrat, [is] creeping
Around by the wall. [He] is a broken-hearted
Little beast. He whimpers and cheeps
All the night, trying to make up his mind to
Run into the middle of the room. But he
Never gets there.*

—Rikki-Tikki-Tavi
Rudyard Kipling

The mares turned their heads and necks indolently toward the approaching Jeep, as Gallagher advanced the four-wheel-drive vehicle through the fresh snow in the long lane and progressed steadily toward the antebellum farmhouse on this cold winter Saturday. Misty vapors emanated from the backs and nostrils of the horses while they yanked frozen timothy from the lean-to hayrack on the back of the barn. The chuck wagon was arriving, but until it produced some apple and alfalfa treats, Josie and Roxie had better fare to attend.

Gallagher eased into the barnyard, and departing the SUV, he made the first human footprints in the area when he stepped toward the hatch to allow Gypsy, his Border Collie, to bound from the cargo compartment.   The hoarfrosted trees throughout the farm created a dazzling contrast with the cobalt sky, and the six inches of white powder that had fallen overnight shrouded the soybean stubs and formed undulating expanses of glistening snow diamonds on the rolling crop fields. The woodpile, bracketed by two walnut trees in the dooryard, was bedecked in snow with a baker's artistry, the white frosting cascading over and down the logs like vanilla icing might festoon the top and sides of a chocolate bundt cake. The snow on the farmhouse, summer kitchen, and horse barn gleamed in the sun, and the roofs seemed to cling to their soft blankets like the morning procrastinator cleaves to his quilts. The black paddock fence formed three drunken shadow lines in the unbroken snow, and a Red-tailed Hawk shrieked while it surveyed the land in its relentless search for the unwary rodent that might poke its furry snout into the frigid air.

Michael Gallagher felt the bite of the fourteen-degree temperature almost immediately, but he would soon accustom to the outdoors after an hour's ride in his toasty Jeep Cherokee. He slipped on his knit hat and pulled up his sweatshirt hood before wiggling into a fleece-lined vest-coat that provided real warmth but allowed for unrestricted arm movement. Once bundled, Gallagher tromped over to the barn where he unlocked the tack room door and then threw open the two main doors to provide the horses access to their twelve-by-twelve-foot stalls. He climbed the haymow ladder and threw down a fresh bail of timothy to stuff into the stall racks. He then grabbed two halters and a lead rope from the tack room and walked to the lean-to stable door on the far left of the barn in order to bring the horses over to the alleyway. Now restrained by only the lift bar across the doorway of the stable, Roxie, the alpha horse, was waiting eagerly in front of Josie in anticipation of the apple-flavored biscuits and alfalfa cubes that she had heard Gallagher toss into the wall buckets. Knowing the drill perfectly, each horse offered her head willingly to the halter to expedite her access to fresh hay and bucket treats.

Gallagher actually resided about forty-five miles from the farm in a mid-sized city where he had been teaching high school English for over twenty-five years. The farm, which he had purchased purely as an investment about fifteen years before, had evolved into a labor of love, and Josie and Roxie, purchased seven and five years before respectively, were ful-filling a dream for Gallagher that dated to his early child-hood. He had not ridden either of the horses since late fall when Jack Hendricks, his farrier, had pulled their shoes and trimmed their hooves for another winter. Once in their stalls, the nascent and ridiculous thought of riding one of the horses through the undisturbed snow around the bridle trail that wound through the ninety acres of crop fields, wood lots, and creek beds began to take hold in Gallagher's mind. His horseback riding was always an exercise in anxiety even in the company of a skilled rider on the most desirable days. The idea of a solo ride on a mid-January day was both pre-posterous and alluring, and even if he did try it, he was not sure which horse he would use. Josie, the twelve-year-old bay at 14.2 hands, was much less imposing to Gallagher, but Roxie, the frisky nine-year-old sorrel at well over 15 hands, was much better trained and a little less spooky.

The smooth snow carpet over the short grass of the bridle trail leading from the barnyard beckoned Gallagher like the sirens called to Odysseus, but Gallagher had no comrades, as the hero of *The Odyssey* had, to blunt the dangerous invi-tation. His only restraints were his inherent fears that for some kind of macho reason he was presently resolved to master. Even those who would urge him to suppress his anxieties would never suggest that he ride alone on a frozen, snow-covered surface. Having, however, seen a colorful pho-tograph in *Farm & Ranch Living* magazine of a rugged cowboy riding a sturdy steed through deep snow while leading a packhorse bearing a Christmas tree, he now imagined him-self on a similar ride. His reluctance in this and other daring matters had often reminded him of Rudyard Kipling's "Rikki-Tikki-Tavi," in which the muskrat, Chuchundra, cowers near the wall at night rather than traverse the room, fearing that the cobras, Nag and Nagaina, might be lurking nearby. Gallagher loathed his restricting aversion to risky adven-tures, and he chafed from his slavish attachment to humdrum security, which as Hecate says in *Macbeth* "is mortals' chiefest enemy."

"What the hell, I'm not gonna live forever," he said in false bravado to Gypsy, who lay in the scattered hay near the stalls with her black and white face resting between her forepaws. She seemed to know intuitively that Gallagher was planning something really stupid.

"Let's do it! Roxie, you're the lucky girl today."

Roxie turned her head from the hayrack in her stall and gave Gallagher a look that virtually said, "You've got to be kidding!"

Fetching a saddle, a blanket, and a bridle from the tack room, Gallagher returned to the alleyway and hooked Roxie to the chain attached to one of the eight-by-eight-inch oak columns that intersected with the barn's crossbeams, using the old-fashioned fork-and-tongue, hole-and-peg connectors. As he brushed and saddled Roxie, Gallagher reflected upon the nature of the crucible before him. This was not a test he had to take; it was not a thesis defense before a graduate committee, nor a speech to parents at an open house, nor a forty-foot barn-roof climb for needed repairs. This challenge he could choose to ignore. It was not the roller coaster ride at LeSourdsville Lake when he was six, the high-dive plunge at Miller's Grove Pool when he was eight, or the prom-date phone call to Megan O'Banion when he was seventeen. While those acts of extraordinary courage were entirely optional, they bore real merit and yielded delightful results (especially the call to Megan), but this was borderline lunacy.

He tightened the cinch a bit more and then swung a leg over Roxie and eased her out of the barn and into the barnyard. Gypsy darted before them, crisscrossing, pirouetting, and yapping in her typically irrepressible enthusiasm. Roxie ignored her for the most part, but the mare would not be averse to taking a shot with a hind hoof at the rambunctious canine if the opportunity arose. Gallagher carefully zigzagged Roxie down the hill from the barnyard, avoiding a direct descent that might cause slippage. He had literally been holding his breath until they entered the bridle path proper and began the second hill that would take them down to the straightaway that led them along the creek meandering through the wood line on their right. Once on the straightaway, Gallagher began singing the theme song from *Sugarfoot,* one of the television westerns he watched as a kid. He had it on good authority that singing to his horses while trail riding sometimes eased their fears and disguised his own, and most of the time it seemed to work. His repertoire of theme songs also included those from *Cheyenne, Maverick,* and *Bronco Layne.*

As they proceeded along the trail, Roxie occasionally turned her head toward Gallagher, seeming to ask if he really wanted to take this ride, but she showed no signs of fractiousness, and she moved ahead with minimal urging. Gallagher's mindset was somewhere between guarded confidence and devout prayer. At length, he began to absorb the surroundings he hoped to enjoy in his private adventure. The land was truly inspiring; everything seemed to glisten in the sun, and the hush that fell over the farm from the fluffy snow and breezeless air suggested a Currier and Ives landscape. He watched a crimson Cardinal light upon a low hanging tree branch that extended over the bridle trial about thirty yards before him. He knew Roxie saw it too, and the bird played Chicken with the horse until it tired of the game and took flight to another perch that Gallagher could not see but the Red-tailed Hawk probably could. In some ways he wished he were sharing it all with someone, but he knew that would defeat his purpose.

At the end of the straightaway, he angled Roxie to the left around a bend and headed back up the farm lane before bearing right into another bean field and on to the bridle trail again. Gypsy continued to dart back and forth and create little snow squalls in her wake, offering an occasional yap or two at nothing in particular. As he started up the gentle grade on the far side of the bean field, Gallagher heard the first and then the second reports from a muzzleloader somewhere beyond the woods to his right, probably on the Ruble property. He had forgotten that Saturday through Tuesday were the four muzzleloader days of a deer-hunting season that would return to a bow-only restriction on Wednesday. He had no sooner said "Keep your eyes peeled for deer" to Gypsy, Roxie, and himself than a 200-pound buck bounded from the woods about twenty yards in front of him on his right and then across the bridle path into the beans. Gypsy barked, and he panicked, but Roxie only slowed and held her course.

"Good girl, Roxie!" he said to the mare as he stroked her neck.

What happened next came from the blue. Roxie had just started forward at a faster pace when she bolted to the left and into the bean field. As she did, Gallagher stayed on for a few yards before he went backwards off the rump of his horse. The ground came up fast and hard, and the rider went down on his shoulder and neck. The pain was instant and blinding, and for about ten seconds, he could feel nothing below his neck and shoulder. *I've got to get up*, he thought wildly, *or I may be paralyzed*. As he did, he ran about ten yards to test his mobility, all the while shaking his right arm to regain some feeling. He became only gradually conscious of Gypsy's hysterical barking and Roxie's frantic whinnying. When he recovered somewhat, he saw Gypsy in a defensive stance and Roxie now snorting and stomping, her reins hanging loosely and dragging. Gallagher then saw the reason for the buck's desperate flight. Five coyotes had quickly formed a rough cordon around the horse, rider, and dog. They had obviously been in pursuit of the buck when in the throes of their hunger they had found easier prey.

"Oh, hell! Now what!"

With military precision, the coyotes began their concentric circling around Gallagher, Gypsy, and Roxie. Gypsy continued her barking while she darted toward and retreated from the coyotes, taking up the defense of man, horse, and herself. Roxie continued to stomp her front hooves, her reins now whipping like fly fishing lines off the sides of her thrashing head. For his part, Gallagher had nothing for self-defense, and his neck and arm were now throbbing from the stinger sustained from the fall. He threw snow at the coyotes, but it was far too powdery to have any effect. As they eased forward, the predators began their low growls and bared their sharp incisors and long canines. Suddenly, two went for Gypsy, and she became a blur in a two-on-one fight that escalated so fast that Gallagher could not react to the mismatch. His head turned involuntarily toward Roxie when she roared, and he watched an airborne coyote the mare had launched perfectly with a hind leg and hoof. When the furry projectile landed about twenty feet away, it whined pitifully and joined a pack mate in a gimpy and tail-between-legs retreat to the woods. As Gallagher turned again toward Gypsy, he saw the fifth coyote advancing toward the outnumbered dog. Gallagher sprang at the coyote and kicked its side, sending it wailing and running across the bean field. With adrenaline pumping, he moved quickly toward Gypsy and threw himself on to one of the coyotes that squirted from his grasp, and the dog's remaining combatant led the coyote twosome in a hasty departure.

Gallagher rolled over on his back in the snow and stared up into the blue sky. He was soon looking into the soft brown eyes of his loving companion, who, with the exception of a few face and ear scratches, seemed none-the-less for the tussle.

"Damn, I love you, Gypsy!"

Gallagher pulled the dog down on to his chest, and she shoved her snout into his neck and shoulder like she did so often on the floor at home. Within a minute he heard the familiar nicker of his other friend who had done herself proud as well. He rose to his feet and walked to Roxie.

Gathering her reins, Gallagher said to the sorrel mare, "Remind me not to rile you, Rox. You're one nasty lady when you get your back up."

He wrapped his arms around her neck and buried his face in her withers. She seemed to know how pleased he was with her.

"I love you too, babe!"

Gallagher swung himself into the saddle and headed back to the bridle path where it soon wound into the woods and out again to where it bordered a fifteen-acre timothy field. After coyote combat, just trail riding, even in snow, seemed like a walk in the park. As he rode, he watched Gypsy before him. Lissome as a willow, she had taken the lead again while keeping him in sight. Her nose to the ground, she was already searching for fun as her jaunty rag tail bounced in rhythm with her gait. Roxie appeared to have formed a discernable respect for her fearless defender who had always yapped and nipped at her from the other side of the paddock fence. Gallagher surmised that a bond had been established among the horse, dog, and man.

Before reaching the horse barn, Gallagher began to reflect on his decision to ride on such a day. Easing Roxie up to the tie post, he looked at Josie in her stall and said, "Well, my dear, you missed quite a ride today." She looked up only briefly before shoving her nose back into the hayrack. Gallagher now began to feel the intense cold again for the first time since before the ride, and he slipped the bridle, saddle, and blanket quickly from Roxie. He handed her a few cubes of alfalfa from a Gatorade cooler on a bench as he brushed her down and then turned her and Josie out behind the barn.

When he walked back into the alleyway, he said to the resting Gypsy, "Well, sweetie, I finally ran into the middle of the room today, and I think old Kipling would be proud of me, but I'd have to tell that muskrat he's right. Nag and Nagaina are out there, and sometimes the snakes beat you and sometimes you beat the snakes. I just don't think I'll test my luck again for a while."

After re-stuffing the hayrack on the back of the barn, Gallagher took Gypsy up to the house and swabbed her scratches with peroxide. She accepted his attentions gratefully and patiently. He then closed up the house and put Gypsy in the backseat of the Jeep. As he started down the long lane for home, he began thinking about that early-April night many years before when he had mustered the courage to call Megan O'Banion and ask her to the senior prom. His gumption today yielded some of the fruits that telephone call provided. The gratification he felt as he returned to the horse barn with his steadfast pals was much like the satisfaction he gained from walking into Wampler's Dance Barn with a prom date his government teacher would tell him the following Monday was "the most beautiful girl at the dance."

Turning from the lane on to the county road, he recalled the smiling image of an ageless girl and thought, *Thank you, Megan, for not dashing my hopes or crushing my spirit as a teenager! Your response to my phone call provides lingering memories of a risk well taken, and it just inspired another. It's a funny thing about pretty girls; you have no way of knowing how your charms will one day be the delight of an aging man's reverie.*

Glancing over his shoulder at the backseat, Gallagher could see that Gypsy had already hunkered down into the blankets that he kept there to protect the upholstery and comfort his pooch. Where else but in the companionship of a faithful dog would he find such unqualified devotion?

"Love ya, Gyps!"

The tail swished a bit, and the ears perked a little, but the eyes remained closed.

The Replacement

There was a cleric from Oxford. [...]
His horse was as thin as a rake,
And he himself [...] was by no means fat. [...]
His overcoat was threadbare. [...]
He spent all he could get [...] on books and schooling, [...]
And gladly would he learn and gladly teach.

—*The Canterbury Tales*
Geoffrey Chaucer

Students would be returning to their dorm rooms on Sunday to begin their second-semester classes the next day, and the anxious headmaster, Dr. Thaddeus J. Spencer, stood looking through the leaded panes of his office window out upon the splendid Dartmore grounds, covered now by snow that had fallen five weeks before and would remain at various depths until mid to late April. He had yet to find a suitable replacement for O'Halloran.

Liam Alexander O'Halloran had collapsed and died in his classroom the day before Christmas break and the semester's end, and his death could threaten the financial stability of staid and storied Dartmore Preparatory. O'Halloran was the quintessence of what had long been one of the most prestigious boarding schools in the East. Prepping at the all-male Dartmore in Aroostook County, Maine himself, he had earned his Bachelor of Arts in English at Bowdoin College and his subsequent Master of Arts in Literature at Princeton University. Widowered twelve years before his own passing, he had sold his home shortly after his wife's demise and taken a room once again at the school, much as he had done for two years as a young and single instructor. He had been one of the few remaining resident teachers, as even the bachelors typically preferred to live off the sixty-acre campus, located about two rural miles outside Presque Isle.

O'Halloran's classroom was a virtual museum of literary history. At his insistence, the desks had been repaired but not replaced in the nearly forty years he had been continuously assigned to the room. Historical maps of England, Ireland, and Scotland spanned large tracts of wall space; and pictures of American, British, German, Irish, and Russian writers were the Rembrandts of a classroom from which the institutional aromas of desk oils and floor cleaners wafted into the hallway. Two pedestals, one in each of the back corners of the room, supported the plaster of Paris busts of Mark Twain and Charles Dickens. Edgar Allen Poe supervised learning from a 24 X 36 poster on the wall above and behind O'Halloran's huge desk. The *piece de resistance* of this mosaic of pictures, paintings, and posters was a framed 16 X 20 copy of the Chandos oil-on-canvas portrait of William Shakespeare. It was mounted on the brick chimney that vented a fireplace of long-discontinued use. Nearby on a plaster wall was an 8½ X 11 sepia copy of Martin Droeshout's portrait of The Bard, as it appeared on the title page of the *First Folio*. The walls were a memorabilia collector's Nirvana.

Added to Spencer's disquiet was the possibility that O'Halloran's death could jeopardize the monetary contributions of Dartmore's most fruitful benefactor, James L. Longstreet, whose youngest and fractious son, Bradley, was expected to graduate in June. Given the current enrollment of approximately 1,000 students, significantly below Dartmore's optimal number of 1,200, revenue from pricey tuitions had plummeted, and the school was relying precariously upon the philanthropy of alumni to supplement lost income. Longstreet was a longtime devotee of the illustrious O'Halloran, who had taught all of the local industrialist's four sons, and the heretofore-reliable patron had suggested to Spencer more than once recently that if ever Dartmore were devoid of an O'Halloran, it would be largely without the pedigree that made it worth the investment. "Thad, if we ever lose the kind of pedagogy and erudition that Liam O'Halloran brings to the classroom, I'm not sure that I and, I believe, others will be as committed to the school."

Spencer had used nearly every weekday during the holidays to interview prospective replacements for the late master teacher, but he had found no applicant with the credentials, presence, or persona who would not pale in comparison with the inimitable O'Halloran. Obviously, a mid-year search was not likely to produce the *crème de la crème* available to step into the position. Some interviewees were eminently qualified on paper but now retired and seemingly drained and lifeless. Others could talk the pedagogical talk, but they were stiff and stoic, most unlike the animated, engaging, and affable O'Halloran. By Wednesday afternoon before the Monday resumption of classes, Spencer still had not settled on a replacement, and the headmaster was a caldron of consternation as he faced not only the problem of finding an instructor for the five English Literature classes but for a dynamism and mastery that would meet the approval of some very discerning alumni.

At two o'clock, Spencer would be interviewing the last of the selected applicants, and the prospects were not favorable. Thomas J. Cahill had hardly been a stellar undergraduate at the rather obscure and low profile Aquinas College in Northern Kentucky, and his graduate work in English at Ignatius University in Southern Ohio was honeycombed with B's. Although his undergraduate coursework was an impressive distribution of sophisticated writing and literature classes, he had taken no teacher education courses and had done no student teaching. Dartmore required no state certification for its teaching staff, but Cahill was a borderline applicant: not qualified for public school teaching and academically most unimpressive for collegiate instruction. When two o'clock had come and gone and the wall clock had chimed 2:30, Spencer began gathering up his stack of applications to review once again before making a decision at home that night over a bourbon and cigar. He had concluded that the last interviewee had decided to bail out on the appointment, rather than make the long drive from Ohio.

At 2:40, however, his secretary, Mrs. Doris Penobscot, knocked on and opened his door to tell him that Mr. Cahill had arrived.

Vexed by the applicant's delinquency, Spencer snapped, "Send him in!"

Mantled in a wrinkled mass of trench coat and toting a tattered mess of manila folders, young Mr. Cahill entered the posh office under a disheveled shock of auburn hair.

"Dr. Spencer?"

"Yes, I'm Dr. Spencer. And I'll guess that you must be Mr. Cahill, although he was supposed to be here forty minutes ago."

"Yes, sir! Well, you see, I've been having some trouble with my car's water pump. It tends to fail after an hour or two on the road, and I have to pull off occasionally and let the engine cool again. I had to stop a few times on U.S. 1. I'm really sorry for any inconvenience I may have caused you."

"I understand. Well, have a chair."

Although Spencer was planning to put young Cahill through some exhaustive questioning, he had already decided that this rumpled, unkempt Irish kid with untamed locks might just be his huckleberry. He realized that looking for an O'Halloran clone was pointless and futile. He needed someone who would replicate O'Halloran's animation but with his own disarming qualities. Now, if this kid could only demonstrate a mastery that was not evident in his transcripts and grade-point averages, he could be just the ticket.

"I see here, Tom, that you've done a little substitute teaching in the fall. Were you not able to find full-time employment in Ohio?"

"Yes. I worked in three high schools, but I found that I was permitted little more than supervising seat work that the full-time teacher had left in his or her absence. Since I didn't take my comprehensives at Ignatius until August, there was very little available in full-time positions."

"How did you learn about the job here at Dartmore?"

"My graduate advisor, Dr. Ackerman, saw it on-line and gave me a call. He said that I ought to fax you my credentials because of your timeline, which I did."

"I must tell you that you'd be replacing the late Mr. O'Halloran, who died suddenly just before Christmas. I must also tell you that he was an institution in and of himself. To say that he was wonderfully well-versed in his subject and highly revered by his current and former students would be a profound understatement."

"I understand."

"You do?"

"Yes. I believe you're telling me that I'd be replacing a near demigod and that what you see before you and in my credentials does not appear very godlike."

At this point, Spencer had to stifle a laugh.

"Yes. Well, it goes without saying that succeeding Mr. O'Halloran, even with considerable advance preparation, would be a challenge. Taking the reins *in media res* for such a personage could be a recipe for disaster in your first time at-bat, so to speak."

"Again, sir, I understand. I don't mean to appear foolishly confident, but I know I can do the job if you'll give me a try. I wouldn't attempt to be Mr. O'Halloran. I know I can't do that. As you can see, I've never sparkled as a student, but I've been told that I have a certain skill in explicating literature. I have no formal training in teaching, but like Justice Potter Stewart's reference to pornography, I know good teaching when I see it."

Again, Spencer had to suppress a laugh.

"Let's talk a little about your studies in English and how you'd begin your work with our students."

For the next hour, Spencer put Cahill through his paces and did what he could to ascertain his strengths. At length, Spencer decided that he had his man, but he did not want to show his hand too soon.

"Tom, do you have a cell phone number where I can reach you?"

"Yes."

"Do you have a room for tonight?"

"Yes. I've booked one at The Pine Tree Inn in Presque Isle."

"Uh...good. I'll call you tonight or tomorrow morning and let you know what I've decided."

On the way out of the office, Cahill asked Doris Penobscot for directions to The Pine Tree Inn and a place where he could get a good dinner. She suggested a small eatery on State Street called The Open Door Grill and recommended the hotshot platter. Cahill piled into his dilapidated Chevy and headed into town, making sure his TracFone was on in case Spencer wanted to contact him immediately with a job answer.

The Pine Tree Inn was straight out of the 1920's or '30's. Its advertising boasted "Fireproof, and Every Room with a Bath." The staircases that led to the rooms were narrow and creaking, and the hallways were dimly lighted tunnels with hardwood floors that pitched and rolled past the mahogany room doors. Entry to the rooms required the patient insertion of timeworn keys, and the door to Cahill's room creaked sharply as he entered. The "amenities" included a black-and-white TV, a vibrating mattress, and a stationary telephone.

By 6:00 p.m., Tom Cahill had showered and changed into his Levi jeans, an Aquinas sweatshirt, and Reebok running shoes. Now famished, he had given up any expectation of a call yet that day from Dr. Spencer. He donned a Cincinnati

Reds ball cap and a fleece lined coat and walked from the Pine Tree on Washburn Road to the Open Door on State Street.

The sign in the window of the Open Door promised "All Home-Cooked Foods," and when he entered, Cahill's cold and reddened nose told his empty and growling stomach that it was in for some tasty restocking. A metal stand just inside the door held the sign: "Please wait to be seated," so he stood as directed until a comely waitress greeted him, asked how many, and then escorted him to a window table that provided an expansive view of State Street. With darkness having fallen, Cahill took momentary note of the quaintness of the town's boutiques and businesses, now in the glow of lamplights that complemented the street's New England ambiance.

"I'm Susan, and I'll be your server. May I start you with something to drink?"

For the first time since he began his trek to Dartmore, Tom Cahill was focused more on something than landing a teaching job. The object of that focus was about 5'8" tall with hazel eyes and thick brown hair that fell to her shoulders. Her gorgeous smile nearly knocked him out of his seat, and her voice was soft but clear. Her pink, waitress dress only partially disguised a stunning body that featured ample breasts, perky buns, and athletic legs. Her nose turned up a bit, and her cheekbones perfected a lovely face. Her gleaming teeth seemed the beneficiaries of skilled orthodontics and regular whitening.

"Uh, sure! Do you have sweet tea?"

"Yes. We do."

"Do you have a raspberry tea?"

Most abruptly, Cahill gained an understanding that this girl would not suffer fools, even if they were patrons.

"No. We don't have raspberry tea, preppy."

Taken aback by her sudden familiarity and pluck, Cahill choked out, "Just the sweet tea will be fine."

Wow, he thought, *she's really something*!

When Susan returned with his tea, she peeled the paper from the straw rather seductively and inserted it slowly into his glass.

"Would you like a menu or just hear the specials?"

"The secretary at Dartmore, Mrs. Penobscot, said I should try the hotshot, but I'm not sure what it is."

"It's thick beef gravy over mashed potatoes and sliced roast beef, next to green beans or your choice of a vegetable. It comes with a fresh, warm roll. You'll like it."

In a pathetically fatuous attempt to extend the conversation, he asked, "Are the potatoes good?"

She gave him a look that practically shouted, "Are you on drugs or just stupid?"

"Do you know what state you're in, preppy? Of course they're good. Do you want the green beans as a veggie?"

Not daring to decline, Cahill offered an exaggerated affirmative.

Susan looked to be somewhere around 20 to 23, and she moved with a confident grace that suggested good breeding and urbane bearing. She brought him his dinner, which was delicious, and despite her tart exchanges, she was very attentive, repeatedly asking if he needed anything. When he finished, she laid the check tray on the table next to his glass and bused his hotshot platter, roll plate, and silverware to the kitchen. Placing a $20 bill on the check tray, Cahill signaled to Susan to take the money. When she brought him his change, Susan thanked him politely and turned to leave his table, but then she hesitated and turned again to face Cahill.

"I noticed that you mentioned Dartmore. Are you a new student there?"

She knew very well that he was not, but she wanted to jerk his chain just a little more.

Irked that she would take him for a high school kid, he blurted, "No! I've applied for a teaching position there, and I just had an interview with the headmaster, Dr. Spencer. I'm staying at The Pine Tree Inn tonight, waiting to hear whether I'll be hired to fill a mid-year English teaching position."

Susan rolled her eyes, and then said, "The Pine Tree!"

"Yeah. It's kind of old fashioned."

Susan laughed a laugh that almost charmed Cahill out of his Reeboks.

"You're not applying for the position that that Mr. O'Halloran held for all those years, are you?"

"Yep."

Again she laughed, this time sympathetically.

"Do you know what a legend he was at the school?"

"Yes. I've been told that very emphatically."

"Well, good luck!"

"In getting the job, or being able to do it."

"Both, I guess. I'm sorry. I've been playin' with ya, a little. I'm a senior in accounting at The University of Maine-Presque Isle." And then with the typical bluntness of a Mainer she asked, "Are ya married?"

"No. No girl with any sense would want an unemployed English major, just out of grad school."

"Don't sell yourself short, preppy. Where'd you go to college?"

"I did my undergraduate work at Aquinas College and my graduate work at Ignatius University."

"I've heard of Ignatius, but where's Aquinas?"

"It's in Northern Kentucky."

"Oh...well, I hope you get the job! If you do, my name's Susan Collins, and I work here three evenings a week on Mondays, Wednesdays, and Fridays. I'm from Houlton, just down the road, and I share a two-bedroom apartment on Chapman Street with another girl who's a biology major at U. Maine-Presque Isle. If you need any encouragement when you get the job, just come in for dinner again."

"When I get the job? You sound a lot more certain than I am. I wasn't very impressive in the interview."

"You'll get it. Wait and see."

As Tom Cahill was making his way in the frigid darkness to the Pine Tree, awash in the mixed emotions of rapture and anxiety, he walked past a dark alley that ran off of State Street. In that alley, a marijuana buy was occurring, the consumer being a handsome young man of about 6'2" and 190 pounds, with wavy blond hair and piercing blue eyes. He was dressed in the most costly of casual attire and wore a Christmas-gifted Rolex watch. He was buying a copious quantity of Vanilla Sky, some of which he would consume himself and the remainder would ensure the loyalty of friends.

At 10:40, Cahill was watching one of the reruns of *Friends* when the room phone rang. Thinking the brusque desk clerk was calling, he answered curtly, "Yeah."

"Tom?"

"Yes!"

"This is Thad Spencer."

"Yes, sir! Good to hear from you!"

"I'm sorry to call you so late and on the hotel line, but I'm at home, and I left your cell phone number in my office."

"Oh, that's okay, really!"

"Well, I decided that there was no point in making you lie awake in anxiety, so I thought I'd let you know my decision tonight."

Spencer paused for what seemed so long that Cahill first thought that he had lost the connection and then that Spencer was struggling to give him the bad news.

"Tom, would you accept the position at the rate of a $44,000.00 annual salary, plus benefits, of course?"

Cahill was dumfounded by the approach. Spencer was not only offering him the position but also a salary amount.

"Uh, sure! Absolutely!"

"You understand that the actual remuneration will be half the $44,000.00 salary because you'll only be under contract for one semester, initially."

"Whatever you say, Dr. Spencer."

"Well, Tom, I'll let you get to bed. I know you must be exhausted. Why don't you sleep in tomorrow and then come to my office around 10:30. Mrs. Penobscot will have a contract ready for you to sign, and I'll give you the keys to your classroom and get you oriented a bit. As you know, classes begin Monday. You'll need to hit the floor running."

"I'll be there, Dr. Spencer! I can arrive earlier if you'd prefer."

"No, that won't be necessary. And Tom..."

"Yes."

"Welcome aboard! I'm really glad to have you!"

"Yes, sir! Thank you very much! I'll see you in the morning!"

"Good-night!"

On Thursday, Cahill arrived at Dr. Spencer's office promptly at 10:30. After signing his contract and multiple employment forms, he toured some of the facilities with Spencer, including the classroom, Room 222. Spencer gave him the keys, the instructor textbooks, the class lists, and O'Halloran's lesson plans.

"Tom, I'm going to let you alone now. Just take this time to familiarize yourself with the room and the building. You're welcome to make any changes to the seating arrangement and the décor, but I'd suggest that you leave things pretty much as they are for the time being. I think that the fewer adjustments the students have to make will be beneficial to you."

"Oh, I'll leave everything as is, Dr. Spencer. I know I've got to prove myself before I take any liberties."

"Don't feel too restricted, Tom. I want you to be your own man. I'm only suggesting that you ease into your role a bit."

"Yes, sir. I understand."

"I'll be in my office for the rest of the day today and all day tomorrow. Just come over if you need something."

"Thank you! I will."

Cahill had called his parents the night before to advise them that he had been given the job and that he would remain in Presque Isle until spring. They would send more clothes and belongings as soon as he had an address.

As Tom Cahill examined his surroundings in Room 222, he began to feel the force of Liam O'Halloran's lingering presence. The room was still his in virtually every way: the ambiance, the desk arrangements, and the wall mountings. What struck and discomfited Cahill some was the copy of the Chandos oil-on-canvass of Shakespeare affixed to the chimney in a direct line from the back of the room to the teacher desk. It seemed that O'Halloran would be watching his every effort through the eyes of Shakespeare. Even now, it was saying, "Don't fail me in your teaching. I'll know if you've gone astray."

After about an hour and a half in the classroom, Cahill packed up the textbooks, class lists, and lesson plans to review that night. Mrs. Penobscot was to make appointments for him to consider three furnished apartments that afternoon. He picked up the appointment times, locations, and directions on his way out and headed for the first apartment visit, scheduled for 2:00 p.m. Since he had had nothing but the orange juice and Egg McMuffin at McDonald's on the way to Spencer's office, he hit Mickey D's again quickly for a Big Mac and fries and ate them in his car in the parking lot.

All three of the apartments were one-bedroom only, but the rent amounts were well within what he had told Penobscot he could afford. The first was on Blake Avenue; the second on Chapman Street; and the third on Epworth Avenue. All were much the same, with a small kitchen and dining area and a living room that would accommodate his needs. The bathrooms were spotless, but the toilets, sinks, and showers looked like World War II-era facilities. The kitchens, bedrooms, and living rooms provided clean but timeworn furnishings, and each apartment had a laundry room in the basement with coin-operated washers and dryers. Notwithstanding the similarity of the three apartments, he chose the second one for a rather compelling reason, its being on Chapman Street. He wrote a check for the six-month deposit and headed to the supermarket for a week's worth of staples.

On Monday morning, Cahill drove on to the campus of Dartmore Preparatory at 7:15 and pulled into the staff parking lot adjacent to E. B. White Hall, the Collegiate Gothic structure that housed the humanities classrooms. It was in perfect harmony with the other buildings, and it epitomized the grandeur, history, and solemnity of this citadel of tradition.

Cahill had prepared zealously for three days to be fully familiar with O'Halloran's plans for the second semester. He would begin the third quarter with the study of poets from the Romantic Period: Burns, Gray, Blake, Wordsworth, Coleridge, Byron, Keats, Shelly, and Lamb. He would finish the third quarter with the essays, poems, and reflections of the Victorian Era writers: Macaulay, Carlyle, Newman, Arnold, Tennyson, the Brownings, and Ruskin. He would devote the fourth quarter to readings from Kipling, Conrad, Lawrence, Joyce, Chesterton, Hardy, Houseman, Yeats, and Thomas. His first and second period students comprised his two Advanced Placement English Literature classes. Third period was his plan time, and fourth was the first of his three regular English Literature classes. After lunch, fifth and sixth periods would also be regular English Literature classes. All went well until sixth period.

Having introduced himself to his sixth period class, Cahill took the roll and then proceeded with an overview of the third and fourth quarters' material. In the middle of his discussion, a brash young man who, without raising his hand to be called upon, simply blurted, "Mr. O'Halloran wouldn't make us read all this crap." A number of his classmates sniggered and grinned at his impudence and cheek.

Stunned, Cahill explained that Mr. O'Halloran's plans for the second semester were quite clear and that they included exactly what had been mentioned so far. The rude student made no further comment but maintained a surly look that foretold future trouble for the new teacher. Toward the end of the class session, Cahill assigned the reading for the next day's discussion and then delineated the requirements of the research paper, a ritual for seniors and due in April. The paper could relate to any writer, work, or movement that had been or would be studied during the year. Students in all of Cahill's classes had until a week from Friday to submit a brief statement of their paper's topic.

About five minutes after the end of class, the rude student returned, and without comment he handed his research paper topic to Cahill: a critical analysis of Mary Shelley's *Frankenstein*. The student was about 6'2" and 190 pounds, with wavy blond hair and piercing blue eyes. His name was Bradley Longstreet.

Over the next few weeks, Cahill directed analyses of the Romantic Period, its ramifications and principal writers. Discussions went well in nearly all classes, as the facility and ease with which he acknowledged his own blunders and laughed at himself won the good will of most students. His Socratic approach to learning encouraged students to analyze and explicate the meanings of poems that would otherwise have been obscure and elusive.

By the deadline or before, all students had submitted their research paper topics, and many were checking with Cahill periodically in regard to some issue or problem. An exception to that practice was Brad Longstreet's. He made no contact with Cahill regarding his paper, and he continued his sullen ways during classes, seeming to grow more recalcitrant as Cahill made inroads with other students. On one occasion Brad made a lewd response to an open-ended question about Keats' "Ode on a Grecian Urn." His confederates chuckled, but most of the others offered disgusted groans and expressions. Cahill had the good sense to let Brad stew in his own juices rather than rebuke him for the impropriety.

Winter lingered over the land interminably in Northern Maine, and by mid March the relentlessly freezing temperatures and ceaselessly overcast skies created a gloom that subdued the spirits of even the most resilient Mainers. Term papers would soon be due, and the tedium of close-grading them would be oppressive. Although Dr. Spencer checked with him regularly and offered support and encouragement, Cahill was often plagued and beset by feelings of Liam O'Halloran's hovering presence. Sometimes, while grading essays or quizzes on late afternoons at the teacher desk, he would feel O'Halloran's judgmental eyes upon him through the Chandos Shakespeare.

Each day offered the hope, however, that during the drive to or from Dartmore he might see Susan Collins on Chapman Street, entering or leaving her apartment. He knew only that she lived on Chapman with a fellow student at U. Maine-Presque Isle. He had not gone to the Open Door since that first night, thinking his motive would be all too transparent. Brief as it was, his experience with Susan absorbed him, and only his busy days kept him from complete preoccupation with her. Before falling asleep at night, he could still hear the lilt of her voice and laughter and envision the curves of her body and the loveliness of her face.

The third quarter ended in mid March, and, owing to the student's abysmal quiz and essay grades, Cahill had no choice but to give Brad Longstreet a D- for the term. He waited for a call from Dr. Spencer or Mr. Longstreet during spring break. It did not come.

Bradley Longstreet showed no signs of dismay or caution when April arrived and the fourth quarter was in full progress. He maintained his surly bearing and bawdy asides during every class. Research papers came due on the 10th, and at the end of class Brad proudly deposited his on Cahill's desk along with the others. Some students had previously asked for and been granted an extension until Monday. The dual burden of class preparations and research-paper grading would now begin for Cahill. As directed, each student had dutifully run the gauntlet and retrieved the witch's broom, and it was now on the desk of the wizard.

By late April Cahill had befriended a few of the single teachers and younger married guys, and he had agreed to join them on a Friday night at the local watering hole, The Beer Barrel Saloon. When he arrived at 7:30 p.m., the place was packed, but Gary Vaughn, a history teacher and football coach, hailed him from the bar and then muscled him into a space that really was not there. Cahill was well into one of his classroom horror stories around 9:30 when an alluring voice behind him cut through the din and said, "Hey, preppy, I didn't think you'd last this long." It was Susan Collins, and he almost dropped his mug of Bud.

Susan was in a pair of Cruel Girl stretch denims and a red turtleneck top, and they accentuated every curve of her body. She was wearing eye shadow and lip-gloss that she did not need, but they made her seem even sexier and more dangerous. She was standing next to a very attractive blond girl, and the two of them were dynamite together.

"This is my roommate, Stacy Kopf. Stacy, this is Tom Cahill, and he teaches English during the day and moonlights in quality control for Maine potatoes."

Stacy leaned into Susan and said, "Like I didn't know that. You've been talkin' about 'im for months."

"Shut up!"

Cahill greeted both girls warmly, but he was nearly in shock, both by the serendipitous meeting and by Susan's recall of his name and type of employment. Throughout the evening, Cahill and Susan became increasingly engaged in *tête-à-tête* conversation, and he eventually revealed that he had chosen an apartment on Chapman because of her and that he looked for her every time he drove down the street. She wrote her apartment address and cell phone number on a bar napkin and made sure he put it in his wallet. She told him that Stacy was leaving for Fort Kent in the morning to spend the weekend at home. Susan invited him to dinner on Saturday night.

The dinner with Susan proved emotionally intimate and splendidly physical. After some very satisfying pasta and a bottle-and-a-half of white zinfandel, Cahill and Collins caressed each other on the way to her room, and they spent the night in semi-buzzed but genuine affection. Lying side-by-side in a state of complete delight in each other, Cahill asked Susan, "How'd you know I was gonna get the job?"

Susan laughed a low, almost wicked laugh and con-fessed, "Thad Spencer is my uncle, my mother's brother. He called me after your interview and told me you were headed to the Open Door for dinner and that he was probably going to hire you as the replacement for O'Halloran. He said I could have some fun with you but not to tell you that he and I were related."

"I'll be damned!"

Cahill left early enough on Sunday to avoid notice and spent most of the day grading papers and text-messaging Susan on his new smart phone. He had never been so cap-tivated by a girl in his life. She was bright and gorgeous, but mostly she was caring, playful, and warm.

The next few weeks of Cahill's teaching were much the same as the others, except that he was now in the throes of tedium and fatigue, balancing class preparations of Modern English prose and poetry with late-night research-paper grading. In an effort to remain focused, he would sometimes return to 222 after dinner to prepare for the next day's class-es and to grade as many research papers as his energy and patience allowed. While that environment kept him on-task, he continued to be haunted and troubled by the unshakable presence of O'Halloran, who watched and evaluated him relentlessly through the disturbing eyes of the Chandos Shakespeare.

Since Susan worked Fridays at the Open Door, on a mid-May Friday evening, Cahill had gone back to his classroom to grade research papers, hoping to have some Saturday free time to spend with Susan, who would be graduating from U. Maine-Presque Isle in early June. One of those papers was Brad Longstreet's, which he had delayed grading for some intuitive reason. By 11:00 p.m., he was wading into Brad's paper and quickly detected sophistication that all but screamed plagiarism. Using a convenient search engine on his classroom computer, Cahill found the entire paper on-line. No wonder Brad had submitted his topic immediately and had raised no questions nor discussed any problems.

What could he do? The obnoxious son of the school's most prolific donor had lifted every word of his research paper from the Internet, and Cahill had printed off a hard copy as material proof. Tom Cahill was both tormented and exhausted. He decided to recline on O'Halloran's massive desk and use a stack of papers for a headrest. As he did so, he pondered his options: confront the cheater and risk a job-ending reprisal from the old man or ignore the falsification and live with the guilt of his craven response. He turned his heavy-eyed face to the Chandos Shakespeare, through which O'Halloran was saying, "I'm watching." Cahill fell into a troubled sleep, and when he opened his eyes again, the sun was breaking through the windows on this beautiful spring morning in Aroostook County, Maine. He swung his feet over the side of the desk and placed his hands on his knees. *Update your resume,* he thought. *You're about to commit professional suicide.* He had decided he would give the paper an F that would fail Brad for the semester. Since Dartmore required four full credits in English to meet graduation specifications, Brad would not receive a diploma in June. Cahill gazed questioningly at the Chandos Shakespeare, and for the first time it offered optimism: "You've arrived, Thomas J. Cahill. If you survive your decision, this classroom is yours."

By mid May, Cahill was sharing most everything with

Susan Collins, especially his problems with Brad Longstreet. On Saturday, however, he decided to tell her nothing about the paper and his decision. She was facing final exams the next week, and she needed no distractions. With Susan deep in study on Sunday, Cahill resolved to complete a marathon grading of the remaining research papers and return them to his students on Monday.

Monday morning's classes were torturous to Cahill, owing to his fixation on the cataclysm that would likely occur during sixth period. By the end of fifth period, however, he had pretty much steeled himself for Brad's reaction, that strength evolving to some extent by the groans of other students who had received lower-than-anticipated grades. As with previous classes, he told his sixth period class that he would return research papers at the end of the period and after a discussion of James Joyce's "Eveline." The most addled Cahill could not have missed the smug look on Brad Longstreet's face that flaunted his confidence in a very favorable research-paper grade, and it intensified the teacher's anticipation of a student meltdown. Near the end of class, Cahill prefaced his return of the papers with some clarifications of his grading system. Settling on a discreet distribution, Cahill called each student's name to retrieve his paper and then depart the classroom. Avoiding a conspicuous delay of Brad's paper, Cahill had placed it near the middle of the stack.

The last student had hardly cleared the doorway before Cahill's peripheral vision told him Brad's large frame had re-entered the room. He was somewhat taken aback by the student's deferential approach.

"Mr. Cahill, I don't get this. There's no corrections on my paper, just an F at the top of the first page."

"Brad, do you want me to tell you that I believe you cheated?"

"Whadya mean?"

"Your paper is plagiarized."

"No, it's not!"

"Brad, don't make me embarrass you any further."

The student stepped closer to Cahill in a more imposingly physical way.

"You embarrass me and you'll hear from my old man, damned soon."

"Okay, then. I'll just let you take this with you to read in private."

Cahill handed Brad a copy of what he had printed from the Internet.

Without further comment, Brad snatched the papers and stormed out the door, leaving Cahill with the expectation of a contentious conference with Dr. Spencer and Mr. Longstreet or, more likely, a threatening call from the power-wielding industrialist. Neither was forthcoming.

By the end of class on Wednesday, Cahill was a bucket of bewilderment. Brad was a smoldering but subdued pupil; however, neither the headmaster nor the father had offered any response to date. That evening, Cahill picked up Susan at the end of work because her old Wrangler was in the service center for repairs. On the way to his car, Cahill finally told Susan about Brad's research paper and the grade he had given him. Walking past the alley where the marijuana deal had been going down in December, they heard an angry exchange emanating from the dark. Cahill told Susan to wait on the sidewalk while he ran down the alley to where he thought he could hear Brad Longstreet's voice. When Cahill reached the dustup, Brad was fending off two thugs who were cursing and punching him. Ignoring his penchant for diplomacy, Cahill jumped into the fight swinging, and Brad, emboldened by the assistance, began throwing upper cuts and right crosses that sent the assailants running.

Collecting themselves, Cahill and Brad walked in quiet discussion to the sidewalk where Susan was in a panicked state.

"It's okay," Cahill assured her under a swelling cheek and

upper lip.

"Okay! You don't look okay. Who's this?"

"This is Brad Longstreet, and he had a little trouble with some street vendors who were questioning his reasons for refusing some Florida property. That right, Brad?"

"Uh...yeah."

"Brad's also one of my students who thinks very little of me."

"I'd say that Brad oughta be kissin' your ass right now."

"No. I think he'd rather be kickin' my ass right now."

Brad had heard enough. "No! Wait a minute. I've got no beef with you, Mr. Cahill. You've put up with a lot of my crap this winter. I didn't wanna like you because I missed Mr. O'Halloran so much. The other guys tried to tell me you were all right, but I just had my head up my ass. I know you had to give me an F on my...that research paper, and I'm okay with the consequences. I'm gonna drive home now and get cleaned up before I head back to the dorm. I'll tell my dad about the paper and how I've acted in your class. You'll see a change in me. I promise."

"And how about that marijuana habit, Brad? It's dangerous in so many ways. You can take an English Lit class online this summer and receive your diploma when you're finished, but this marijuana crap is dead serious."

"I know. There's a whole lot of stuff I've gotta change, but I don't want you to change, Mr. Cahill. You need to stay at Dartmore next year. That junior class needs you!"

"Thanks, Brad, but that's up to Dr. Spencer."

Brad walked toward his car but turned and waved.

Susan elbowed Cahill in the ribs and said, "I think I kinda like you, preppy." She put her arms around his neck and kissed his lips tenderly. "Now take me home. I've gotta study."

On Friday after his last class, Cahill had a sitdown with Dr. Spencer and Mr. Longstreet. They discussed Brad's options. Spencer, for prudent reasons, granted permission for Brad to walk in commencement and receive a blank diploma, all very discreetly. Brad would take English Literature on-line to meet graduation requirements. After Longstreet left, Spencer told Cahill to stay. "Tom, I want to renew your contract for next year. You've done a stellar job for us. What do you think?"

"I'm all yours if you'll have me!"

"Done then."

At Susan's graduation from U. Maine-Presque Isle in June, she introduced her parents to Cahill. "Mom and Dad, this is Tom Cahill. He's in potatoes."

Mrs. Collins laughed and said, "We've heard all about you, Tom, and we're really glad to meet you!"

Within two weeks, Susan had a job offer in accounting for a corporation just up the road in Caribou, and she would begin preparations for her Certified Public Accountant exam. She and Tom were also making preparations for an incorporation of their own.

The Day Will End

Delaney wheeled his Ford Bronco into the staff parking lot of Walt Whitman, the small junior-senior high school in an Appalachian district in Southern Ohio. During the nine-mile drive from the farmhouse he was renting, he navigated the dank mid-March mist and gloom that hung over the frosted stubble in the rolling acres of soybeans and field corn along the county road. Such a morning and terrain put him in mind of what he imagined the moors of Yorkshire and Dartmoor, England to be when he read them described in nineteenth century British novels and short stories.

Doyle Delaney was nearing the end of his first year as a secondary principal after twelve years as an English teacher in a large suburban high school in Central Ohio. He had reluctantly accepted the administrative position in mid August at the repeated request of the local superintendent and the vigorous urging of his doctoral advisor at the university. While he knew the job would be a learn-as-you-go experience, he had not anticipated such a baptism of fire.

"Another day in paradise," he uttered sardonically, as he exited the SUV at 7:10 a.m. and looked across the gravel expanse to see if the lights were on in the trailer that served as the central office for a school district that also included two antediluvian K-6 elementaries, east and west of the junior-senior high. John Stoeckline, Delaney's superintendent, was an imposing man at 6'5" and 265 pounds, with a thick shock of wiry salt-and-pepper hair, but he was typically quite serene and thoughtful, as many country educators were. That laid-back approach included a rather casual view toward his own arrival time. The trailer was still dark, meaning that neither Carol Moore, the treasurer, nor Alice Land, the secretary, had arrived as yet.

Delaney entered the side door of the building off the parking lot, and he knew immediately that Grover Stemple, the school's custodian, had arrived at 5:30 to stoke the boilers and have the place cozy by 7:00. As he turned the corner of the main hallway, Delaney nearly collided with Stemple, who was wearing his characteristically petulant game face. Grover was not a morning person. He was not an afternoon or an evening person either, but mornings were an especially hazardous time to encounter this irascible but resourceful, multi-talented, and indefatigable custodian.

"Those damned kids stole another one of the shower handles from the boys' locker room yesterday! I took the last one off and put it in the lap drawer of your desk. You can let Scott use it to turn all the showers on and off after each P.E. class."

Delaney knew that the showers were so old that handle replacements were hard to find and that Grover had every right to be vexed, but the neophyte principal drew upon every measure of self-restraint to suppress a playful laugh at a major instructional issue in the boondocks.

"All right. I'll tell Scott that if he loses it, he'll have to update his resume."

"Uh...yeah!" said the mirthless Grover, for whom subtleties were often a perplexing vagary if not an inscrutable riddle.

Delaney unlocked the outer door of the main office, and

then he checked his mailbox before opening the door to his own space.

"No messages. It's gonna be a great day!"

Delaney's administrative experiences had often harkened him to one of the lines from Shakespeare's *Julius Caesar* that he enjoyed reading with his sophomores back at Wickfield High School: "Oh that a man might know the end of this day's business ere it come! But sufficeth that the day will end, and then the end is known."

Delaney turned down the radiator behind his desk and plopped into the leather swivel chair that had borne the weight of many beleaguered principals' tired backsides. He figured that it had to have been a class-gift to Walt Whitman Junior-Senior High School from guys who were about to do battle with the Kaiser. As he reviewed his desk-calendar notes, Rhonda Richardson, his secretary, came into the outer office, stowed her coat and purse, and then stuck her head into Delaney's office.

"Morning!" she practically sang in her typically ebullient manner.

"Hiya."

If he lived to be a hundred, Delaney would never understand what could make anyone so damned upbeat at 7:30 in the morning.

Rhonda was the quintessential country girl who at twenty-seven had two daughters in diapers whom she deposited each morning at her mother's farmhouse. Her hair was long, black, and straight; she was a little wan, but she exuded femininity with minimal cosmetic assistance. At about 5'8" she was not a pound over 125, and she was always perfectly groomed and coiffed. Her dresses were never flashy but always perfect for her figure. A quick study, she was punctual, efficient, and observant; often identifying a volatile situation for Delaney before it erupted. She practiced a work ethic drawn from a childhood on a cattle-and-grain farm and a marriage to a farmer who owned only fifteen tillable acres but worked 300. She carried much of the financial load for her husband, Mike, and their children; her employment with the school district provided a family-plan health insurance policy. She had preceded Delaney in her position at the high school by only one month, but as a graduate of Walt Whitman, she understood the lay of the land and the will of the people. Delaney knew that without her he would have lasted less than a week, but if he were to give voice to that thought, people would think him a braggart.

After morning announcements made on a public-address system as cantankerous as Grover Stemple, Delaney was about to make his rounds in the building to usher any Monday morning stragglers to their rooms and assure himself that all classes were well under way. Into his doorway stepped Carson Spears, the Vocational Agriculture teacher, and his expression foretold the tenor of the message.

"Uh...we've got a little problem in the parking lot."

The Vo-Ag classes were to have already departed on a field trip to Ohio State University, and Spears, who held a chauffeur's license, was to be driving the school bus and conducting the excursion.

"What kind of 'little problem'?"

"Tyler Taylor's out there in his dad's Camero, and he's drunk as a lord. He's supposed to be goin' with us."

"Lead the way."

When Spears and Delaney reached the car, Delaney found the student with his head resting against the seat and his face as green as a John Deere combine. Spears opened the door, and a nearly empty bottle of Jack Daniels rolled out on to the gravel.

"Mr. Spears, would you bring Tyler into my office while I give his parents a call."

Carson half lifted the portly student out of the driver's seat, and in a round-about manner he guided him into the building and down the hall to the main office. The dutiful teacher maneuvered the staggering student into a visitor's chair across from Rhonda's desk while Delaney called the boy's house from his desk phone. Delaney knew that the student handbook stated an automatic five-day suspension for anyone under the influence of alcohol or a controlled substance on school grounds, and he figured he would be facing stiff parental resistance to the penalty.

"Hello."

"Taylor residence?"

"This's Brad Taylor."

"Mr. Taylor, this is Doyle Delaney, principal at Walt Whitman, and I have Tyler here in the office."

"No, ya don't. He's on a Vo-Ag field trip this mornin'.'"

"Well, yes, he was supposed to be, but Mr. Spears found him intoxicated in your car in the parking lot this morning, and I'm afraid I'll have to ask you or your wife to come over to school and get him."

"Had a few too many, did he?"

"Well, yes sir, but under handbook regulations, I'll have to suspend him for five days, beginning immediately."

"Well, I'll put him to work around the farm after he does his school work each day."

"While I encourage you to keep him in touch with his studies, please know that for the five days he'll be out of school, he'll take zeros on all assignments due and all quizzes and tests administered during that time period."

"Now you jist wait a friggin' minute. You ain't given him zeros in nothin'. I'm comin' up to that schoolhouse now!"

Carson Spears left Tyler with Rhonda and went to the parking lot to get the bus rolling to Columbus. Meanwhile, the rotund Tyler turned greener and greener while Delaney reviewed the handbook for any ambiguities regarding student intoxication on school grounds. As Delaney stepped into the doorway of his office to check on Tyler, the closed, bottom half of the Dutch-style door of the main office flew open violently and slammed loudly against the wall. Stepping boldly into the office was a ruddy-faced hulk that stood about 6 feet tall and weighed about 280 pounds. He was country dapper in bib overalls over a grimy flannel shirt that was rolled to the elbows and revealed forearms that made Popeye's look like Mr. Before's.

"You Delaney?"

Delaney looked reflexively at his secretary in the vain hope she would answer to that hateful name, but her expression clearly said, "You're on your own this time, Bub!"

Desperate to avoid a voice in three higher octaves, Delaney responded, "Yes, I'm Doyle Delaney. Are...are you Mr. Taylor?"

"That'd be me."

"Well...as you can see, Tyler is very intoxicated, and I think the best course would be for you to take him home now, and I'll give you a call later to discuss the consequences."

"Consequences, my ass!"

With that, Brad Taylor put one knee down in front of his son's chair and lifted the boy's face into his. Glancing over his shoulder, he barked at the principal, "Why, he ain't drunk! He's jist sick from that cold medicine his mama give 'im this mornin'."

Delaney started to respond, but before he could offer his rebuttal, Tyler offered it for him, "Aaagghhh...aaagghhh."

Tyler refuted his dad's asinine defense by heaving nearly a full pint of pure sippin' whiskey down the bib and into the pockets of Brad's smartly distressed OshKosh B'Goshes.

Brad Taylor turned to Doyle Delaney with the most dumbfounded look on a full-grown man the principal had ever seen. Delaney did not allow himself even the hint of smile.

To his cherished progeny, Brad offered his judicious censure, "Why you, dumb sumbitch!"

Brad jerked the beefy Tyler out of the chair like a twenty-pound sack of Idaho Reds and wheeled him toward the door. He then plunged a size-12 Red Wing into his son's bulbous buttocks that sent him lurching through the doorway and into the hall. After that, the male bonding between father and son became dramatically animated on the way to the parking lot.

Rhonda looked up calmly and said wryly to the astonished Delaney, "I guess Brad'll be okay with that suspension now. Should I get the forms ready?"

All Delaney could provide for response was caustic laugher all the way to his desk chair, but his fingers were still trembling.

Delaney spent the remainder of the morning working on two of the five teacher evaluations he needed to complete before April. Board policy required him to complete a comprehensive evaluation of each veteran teacher every four years. Those new to the staff required a comprehensive evaluation for the first two years and then every four years thereafter. The comprehensive format mandated two formal observations in the first semester, followed by a written, mid-year evaluation; and two formal observations in the second semester, followed by a final evaluation to be signed by the teacher and submitted to the superintendent in time for the April board meeting. Delaney was far behind schedule, so he had worked all morning on the reports, and then he returned to his desk immediately after lunch to remain on task.

At 1:20, Rhonda came to his door to tell him that Sandra Daugneaux had sent Bitsy Scott to the office with a note for him to read. Bitsy was one of the buck-toothed, sassy-mouthed twins who could keep one principal busy all day. Fractious and bellicose to say the least, Bitsy and Betsy were absolutely identical, and they never missed an opportunity to exploit their similarities and misrepresent their identities. Indeed, they had more than once made Delaney the prince of fools by assuming each other's name. Ms. Daugneaux was the cranky, eighth-grade social studies teacher whom almost all the students and some of the staff called "Dog Nuts."

"Send her in."

Having read Daugneaux's note as Bitsy stood defiantly next to his desk, Delaney asked the question that invited not only the predictable answer but also facilitated his understanding of the local vernacular.

"Bitsy, Mrs. Daugneaux says here that you took advantage of her when you asked for a restroom pass and then took over a half an hour to return to class. Why'd you take so long?"

Leaning forward for emphasis and with her fists buried in her ample hips, the equally offended and indignant Bitsy bellowed, "Ah haad ta turrrd!"

In that succinct explanation, the erstwhile English teacher learned that a certain slang reference to scatological matter could serve as an infinitive as well as a noun.

Delaney sent Bitsy back to class and put a note in Sandra's mailbox, asking her to see him in the morning during her plan period to discuss some strategies for the B & B twins. Returning to his evaluations, he lost all track of time until the 3:15 bell rang to end the school day. After the buses had cleared the parking lot and most of the staff had exited the building around 3:45, Delaney returned to the main office to go over some items with Rhonda before she left at 4:00.

Winking at him puckishly while handing him some telephone messages from the county office and the joint vocational school, Rhonda opined, "Well, you've learned a little more today about country education, haven't you, Mr. Principal."

"Yeah, and to think I dropped a bundle on degrees when I could've just roamed the hallways here for a few weeks."

"But just think of the perks: the mac 'n cheese lunches, the front-row seats at class plays, the stimulating conversations with students and parents..."

"Go on home to your kids. They might think you're funny."

"I will. You're just a grumpy old man!"

Rhonda cleared her desk and gathered up her things. She would be ready for just about anything that came her way in the morning. At 4:05, she leaned into Delaney's office and said, "See you tomorrow. Go home and get some rest."

"Thanks, kid! You too."

Delaney could hear Rhonda lock the outer door as she left, so he thought he could concentrate for a while on the evaluations. At about 4:30, however, he heard the outer office telephone ringing, but he knew that John Stoeckline had left his office, so he decided that whoever was calling could wait until morning. But when the ringing continued, he thought the caller might be Rhonda trying to remind him of something important.

"Walt Whitman High School."

"Delaney?"

"This is Doyle Delaney."

"Jist wanna let ya know that when ya come through town, we're gonna kick the shit outta ya."

Delaney believed the caller to be Lonny Scroggins, the seedy parasite who lived with the mother of the six Robinson kids, the oldest of whom, 19-year-old Justin, Delaney had recommended for expulsion in January. John Stoeckline acted upon the recommendation unhesitatingly. Scroggins, who was strung-out most of the time, had decided he would take up the honor of the Robinson name and threaten Delaney with ominous phone calls. This time, he not only sounded drunk again, but Delaney could hear other male voices in the background. Scroggins had once done eighteen months in the slammer for attacking a guy in a service station with a monkey wrench.

Walt Whitman Junior-Senior High School was located at the end of a dead-end street, and the only way out of the flashing-red-light of a village was through the four-way stop that had a gas station on one corner, and a hardware store, a food mart, and a barber shop on the other three. Delaney went to his Bronco and retrieved his tire iron from the cargo area and threw it on the front seat. He then went back into his office and called the county sheriff's office.

"Deputy Radson."

"Uh...yes, Deputy. This is Doyle Delaney, principal down at Walt Whitman, and I've got a potential problem with one of the locals, Lonny Scroggins, who's let me know that when I try to leave school today, he and some others are going to waylay me and work me over. I just want to let you know in advance because I've put my tire iron on my front seat, and I intend to use it to defend myself if they try to stop me."

After a moment's pause, Radson said in response, "Mr. Delaney, you just stay in your office, and I'll take a ride down there directly, but it'll take me about thirty minutes to get there."

"Well I hate to drag you down here, but I could use the help."

"No problem. I haven't run Lonny in for a long time, and he's probably gettin' brash again. Sit tight. I'll see ya in about thirty minutes, maybe less."

Delaney decided that discretion was, in fact, the better part of valor, so he remained in his office until he heard a tap at the outer office door. When he opened it, before him stood a V-shaped deputy in a broad-brimmed hat and an impeccable black uniform.

"Mr. Delaney?"

"Yes, sir. C'mon in."

As the deputy stepped into the outer office, the leather of his gun belt, holster, and boots made that squeaking sound that just exudes authority. Deputy Radson was every inch of 6'4" and at least 235 pounds, and you just knew you did not trifle with this fellow. Shaking hands with Delaney, the deputy was most deferential.

"I'm Deputy John Radson."

"Kinda thought so."

"Well, you were right. When I approached the four-way, I could see a bunch of 'em in the gas station, but they scattered pretty quickly. I did get a good look at Scroggins, though, so he probably made the call. Gimme fifteen minutes before ya leave. I'm goin' back to the gas station and let the word out that I'm lookin' for Lonny and that I've got a little mayhem in mind. Don't think he'll wanna perform in this drama after that."

"I really appreciate your help, but what makes you think Scroggins won't be back at it tomorrow or the next day when you're not here?"

"Lemme tell ya a little story. You mighta heard about Scroggins bein' in the lock-up for attakin' a guy with a wrench."

"Yeah, I did."

"Well, I took the call the night when he was cuttin' loose. He was drunk again, of course, and when I got there, he was in the middle of the intersection swingin' the wrench three-sixty and darin' anyone to come near 'im. But he was so drunk I took 'im down easily, cuffed 'im, and stuck 'im in the back of the cruiser. On the way back to town, he started stompin' the back of my seat with his feet while his hands were cuffed behind 'im. I told 'im ta knock it off about three times before I stopped the car, got out, shot a little pepper spray into the back seat, and went over to the side of the road and sat for a while. It was winter, of course, so all the windows were rolled up. After about five minutes, I opened his door and said, 'Lonny, you 'bout done?' He just looked at me through those blurry eyes and nodded. Lonny has no interest in playin' any games that might involve me as the referee. Truth is, the pepper spray didn't bother 'im as much as it might've if he hadn't been so drunk."

"I guess that'd probably get my attention too. Remind me not to tie one on when you're on duty."

Radson just laughed and slapped Delaney gently on the back.

"In your case I'd probably just make ya listen to some those awful jokes I hear ya tell at staff meetings."

"Those back-stabbin' finks! Who squealed on me?"

"I never betray an informant. Besides, I hear they love ya."

"Oh, yeah."

"Call me whenever ya need me."

As Delaney drove home through the gray, misty twilight, he reflected upon the circumstances in which he had come to be where he was. He had set his wipers on low speed, and the rhythmic swish immersed him in a stream of consciousness that carried him to that late-August day when he was seated on a box of books in the basement of the central office where his interview for a freshman English teaching position at Wickfield High School had just concluded. The assistant-superintendent, Carl Heberling, then offered him the job in a most curious fashion. Opening the master contract to the salary schedule, he directed Delaney's attention to the line that represented his starting salary.

"Mr. Delaney, do you see anything here that would make you want to accept my offer of a job here at Wickfield?"

Heberling was trying to avoid fruitless, further discussion by showing the recent graduate the embarrassing remuneration. The callow Delaney, however, had never dreamed that much money could be his just for doing what he so wanted to do. His naïve delight in that meager starting salary now reminded Delaney of what musician and comedian Phil Harris had said during a pro-am golf tournament when he discovered his bunker shot lying six inches from the cup: "I feel like Sophia Loren's newborn baby when he opened his eyes and said, 'Oh my lord, is all this for me?' " Cracking up, crooner Pat Boone guffawed, "And here I am makin' all these milk commercials!" The young Doyle Delaney, of course, had accepted the position.

He wondered, as he eased his way up the long lane to the remote farmhouse, whether he would see the day when bright and inspired college students would flock to teaching because of the competitive salaries. Maybe.

Movers and Shakers

There was a monk, [...]
Whose job was to supervise the monastery's estates.
And who [...] had many excellent horses in his stable,
And [...] his sleeves edged with fur, the finest in the land;
He was a fine fat lord, and [...]
His boots were supple, and his horse richly equipped.

—The Canterbury Tales
Geoffrey Chaucer

James O'Neill lay on the couch reading the most recent issue of his high school alma mater's quarterly magazine, *Excalibur*. As he did so, he read with particular interest the financial report, delineating the various contributions to Holy Cross High School's annual fund raising. Formerly all-male, now coeducational, the school had merged with its all-female sister school years ago in order to maintain a viable student enrollment that facilitated a comprehensive offering of college preparatory courses, an aggregation of highly skilled instructors, and (perhaps most importantly) a broad distribution of very competitive athletic teams.

O'Neill was intrigued, as he always was, with the compartmentalization of donors and their respective contribution amounts. The categories of contributor classifications comprised alumni, parents, parents of alumni, and friends. The ranking of donors included President ($10,000 +), Regent ($5,000 +), Distinguished ($2,500 +), Laureate ($1,500 +), Sustaining ($1,000 +), Century ($100 +), and lowly Contributor ($1-99), of which he was one of the usual suspects. He often wondered how many of the high-roller donors would be as generous if all contributions were to be made anonymously. True, some of the loftiest donors chose to be listed only as "anonymous," but most of the big-money supporters expected their names to be prominently listed among the upper echelon of alumni movers and shakers. O'Neill was not so naïve as to believe that all institutions, both private and public, did not have to pay tribute to wealthy benefactors in some way. Without doubt, a strictly anonymous method of giving would drastically reduce contributions to any institution.

"Here I go again," he said to himself, knowing that the financial section would launch him into another orbit of ruminations that intensified his emerging belief that the American Catholic Church and its grade schools, high schools, and colleges were predominantly driven by the unbecoming pursuit of influential lucre. As an archetypal product of the very structures he criticized, he was steeped in Catholic doctrine. Baptized into Catholicism shortly after birth and educated in Catholic schools from first grade through graduate school, he had studied and experienced the papal traditions and dogmas in virtually every way and level. He had been an altar boy serving the priests and reciting the Latin responses during pre-Vatican II Masses. He had received all the obtainable sacraments beyond Baptism: Penance, Holy Communion, Confirmation, and Matrimony. Never remotely suited for Holy Orders (a vocation), he was in no hurry to receive Extreme Unction (the last rites). Obliged by undergraduate requirements at Aquinas College, he had taken twelve semester-hours of Catholic Theology courses and eighteen semester-hours of Thomistic Philosophy courses. Still, every time he read some kind of publication that listed the hierarchy of Catholic donors, he hearkened back to his school days when the scions of wealthy industrialists, physicians, lawyers, and speculators were clearly the *crème de la crème* of a school's population.

For the most part subtle, the preferential treatment of

certain well-connected students was clear when viewed from the perspective of the have-nots. Frequently, the manifestation of these underlying accommodations was in the meting out of disciplinary consequences. Again, O'Neill addressed himself, "Oh yeah, I remember that one really well. That snowball caper was a real classic."

About seven or eight of O'Neill's eighth grade male classmates had gathered at noon one icy February day and spent most of the hour bombarding cars with snow- and ice-packed mortar shells from an escarpment on the edge of the school grounds. Both the climbing and descending cars on the steep and adjacent Peach Street were veritable fish-in-a-barrel. The plaintiff telephone calls reached Principal Sister Roberta Anne's office within minutes after lunch. Since the entire group had arrived late to class from their nefarious work, the most addled brain could have discerned the identity of the culprits. Roberta Anne, nevertheless, raised the perfunctory question: "Who was up on that hill throwing snowballs down at cars?" The right or left hand of every miscreant went up but that of Roland Wabler, whose father was a wealthy industrialist and heavy contributor to the parish coffers. Roberta Anne knew, of course, from Wabler's reddened face and late arrival that he had to be among the mortar launchers, but she ignored the obvious and suspended the others for two days. For Jimmy O'Neill that day, his learning moment was not so much that he had paid a well-deserved price for his transgression, but, as he would one day read in George Orwell's *Animal Farm*, "Some animals are more equal than others."

"Yeah, that was one of several awakenings," O'Neill turned on the couch and said to his somnolent Border Collie, Maggie, whose response was to roll from her left side to her right, between the couch and the coffee table. "But there were others that to a greater or lesser degree underscored the special treatment of the chosen. Like that time when I was in the sixth grade and each homeroom had to select a representative to go down to the church annex for a group picture of the Catholic Schools Mission Crusade efforts throughout the world." To this absorbing topic, Maggie yawned and closed her eyes again.

Jimmy O'Neill's name had been drawn from a hat as one of the two sixth-grade homerooms' representatives for the picture, even though his teacher, Sister Maura, emitted a muffled groan when she withdrew his name. The picture was to be taken of two rows of students, the back row on chairs, and they would be holding placards rendering third-world countries, each with a band-aid drawn across the profile of the land. Standing in front of both rows was an eighth grade boy and a fourth grade girl; the boy holding a breviary and attired in a black biretta with purple tuft, a black cassock, and a purple sash, signifying the clerical rank of the parish's pastor, Monsignor Murphy. The girl was garbed entirely in a floor-length black dress and a face-surrounding habit, which were accented by the long wooden rosary of the Sisters of Peace. Interestingly, the boy was the son of one of the most prominent contractors in the parish and a huge donor, and the girl was the boy's sister and the daughter of that same luminary. Obviously, only parish royalty was to wear the raiments of a priest and nun.

"Ya know, Maggie, even as an eleven-year-old, I was struck by the family name and wealth of the two who were selected for such an exalted role."

O'Neill swung his feet on to the floor of the family room, stood up, and shuffled into the kitchen to rescue a Miller Lite from becoming too old or too cold in the fridge. Twisting the cap from the beer bottle, he poured himself a handful of Planters Dry Roasted Peanuts and retreated to the couch. Pulling the *Excalibur* from the coffee table again, he ran his eyes down the lists of donors, recognizing a number of the big bucks people from his Holy Cross graduating class. An inset statement from the current archbishop gave rise to another reason for browbeating Maggie.

"My mom used to get so angry with her best school and life-long friend, Rosie, who was the spinster aunt of the arch-bishop when I was a kid. Mom'd tell me how Rosie would go on *ad nauseum* about dinners with her nephew in his lavish home, featuring the most opulent appointments. 'Appointments' are the fancy trmmin's, girl. Anyway, Rosie would boast of Bishop David's beautiful vestments, and she'd go on at length about the magnificent table settings, the crystal chandeliers, and the sumptuous entrees. Boy, would Mom ever get steamed over the titular head of the archdiocese livin' so high on the hog."

O'Neill flipped through a few more pages of the *Excalibur* and found pictures and an article about a large number of senior students who had gone to Washington, D.C. during their spring break. That was the catalyst for another round of grousing.

"Mags, did I ever tell ya about the time my best friend got to tell our seventh grade homeroom about his summer trip to Philadelphia?"

At this point, O'Neill took another pull on his beer bottle and traveled back to that day in early September of his seventh grade year at Our Lady of Grace Grade School. He had been walking with his class into the building from the playground/parking lot on that first day of the school year when Sister Maura, his sixth grade teacher, accosted him in the hallway and demanded to know why she had not been told that he would be absent from class during the last week of school, the first week of June.

"I felt like a penny waiting for change, young man!"

She must have used that expression 100 times the year before.

When he returned home that day, he exploded on his mom for not advising Sister Maura that he would be absent for the last week of school in the sixth grade. "She bawled me out in front of everybody!"

"I called Sister Roberta Anne, and she told me she'd

advise Sister Maura. She must have forgotten to do so. I'll take care of it."

Jimmy thought his mom treated the situation rather calmly in his presence, but he could hear her later on the telephone discussing the issue with Sister Maura in less than deferential terms.

What was, in Jimmy's mind, much more significant than that humiliation in the hallway was the next day's development in Sister Catherine Anne's seventh grade homeroom. Around two o'clock that day, about forty-five minutes before dismissal, she ended the history lesson and announced, "Class, I have a very educational treat for you. This morning I asked Kevin Kearney to share some of the highlights from his trip to Philadelphia, when he accompanied his father, Mr. Kearney, who was attending a legal conference in one of the nation's most historical cities. Kevin has agreed to tell us about it. Kevin..."

Following that glowing promotion, Kevin Kearney, Jimmy's O'Neill's best friend, marched to the front of the classroom to provide a description of the important Philadelphia edifices, monuments, and offices that fifty cents worth of postcards in a Philly souvenir shop would have rendered much more graphically and picturesquely.

Jimmy did a slow burn as Kevin milked every detail in a center-stage moment for another member of the school's sovereigns. What hurt most, however, was that his trip in the first week of June, for which Jimmy had paid such an ignominious price in the hallway in the first week of September, was to the United States Military Academy at West Point, New York. His oldest brother, who had been a scholar-athlete at Holy Cross High School, named to all-area teams in football and basketball, and received appointments to both the United States Military and Naval Academies, had chosen West Point and gone on to play quarterback for the Black Knights on some of Army's most powerful "Red" Blaik coached teams. Jimmy, along with his family, had traveled to West Point in early June to attend his brother's graduation. Besides visiting one of the most historically significant and magnificently beautiful venues in America, above the Hudson River in the Catskill Mountains, Jimmy O'Neill would have up-close proximity to President Dwight David Eisenhower, the erstwhile Supreme Allied Commander of World War II, who was there to celebrate his fortieth reunion with classmates, provide the commencement address, and greet and hand the diploma to every graduate.

Jimmy had spent June Week at West Point with his parents and other brother, and they watched from the viewing stand the entire Corps of Cadets in a splendid parade on the Plains pass in review before the President. Later in the event, the seniors broke from ranks and assembled in a line as the underclassmen paraded in the traditional "eyes right" tribute past the imminent graduates. Jimmy and his family went to Mass in the Catholic Chapel, attended a garden party with the Superintendent, viewed the amazing battle mural in the cadet dining hall, and stood about ten-feet from President Eisenhower as he walked with a West Point class that "the stars fell upon." They also strolled through the West Point Cemetery and found the marker of George Armstrong Custer.

At graduation in the gymnasium, one of the staff officers approached Jimmy and escorted him to a strategic spot behind the seated graduates. "You stay right here, and I'm pretty sure one of the graduates' white hats will sail right into your hands when they toss 'em in the air." While many in attendance scrambled for the coveted hats, Jimmy proudly rejoined his family with the beautiful white and brass treasure that had landed at his feet. Jimmy kept that hat for the rest of his life.

Before the O'Neill family left West Point after the graduation, Jimmy's dad received a tip that he acted upon quickly. Telling Jimmy to jump in the car, they drove to a tavern in Highland Falls, where they met and talked with at some length the real-life Martin "Marty" Maher, about whose life

Director John Ford had just shot a movie at West Point, *The Long Gray Line*. The movie had been filmed during the recent school year, and many of the marching scenes involved the current cadets. Starring Tyrone Power, as "Marty" Maher, and Maureen O'Hara, as Mary Maher; the cast also included Ward Bond, Betsy Palmer, Donald Crisp, Peter Graves, Harry Carey, Jr., and Patrick Wayne. Sister Roberta Anne would show the rented film in the auditorium to the seventh and eighth graders in the spring of the next year. With his two brothers driving home together, Jimmy traveled with his parents, and they stopped in New York City, where Jimmy and his mom rode to the top of the Empire State Building, and then they all saw from an excursion bus the *Queen Mary*, the *Queen Elizabeth*, and the *Constitution*, which happened to be in port at the same time.

"Mags, I've never been the sharpest knife in the drawer, but over the years I've often suspected that if my dad had been Dr. O'Neill instead of just Francis O'Neill, I might have been asked to tell about a truly significant and timely event to all four of the seventh and eighth grade homerooms."

O'Neill flipped some more pages of the *Excalibur* and found pictures and discussion of the STEMM laboratory that had been recently completed at Holy Cross High School and largely funded through donor contributions.

"Wow, that's damned impressive, Mags! Do you think I've just become a jaundiced and sour old curmudgeon? Don't answer that."

There were some really great teachers in the schools I attended who came into my life at just the right times, he thought. *Young Sister Lela Conroy, who took over for the ill Sister Catherine Anne in January of my seventh grade, relieved my math anxiety and made me feel worthwhile and cherished as a student for the first time in months. She took Matt McGinnis and me under her wing and made us laugh along with her and love coming to school. Standing in the parking lot with her shawl around her one frigid day after school, she cheered and clapped for us vigorously as we roared down the steep, snowy hill, doing wipeouts on an eight-foot, two-by-ten pine board. Loved her!*

Brother James Collins erased all of my Holy Cross High School foibles one day in my American Literature class. "O'Neill," he said in response to my interpretation of some lines from a puzzling poem, "you can be a real scatterbrain, but sometimes ya truly amaze me." He didn't know it, but he had just sown the seeds of my interest in English as an academic discipline. The fact that he'd been an all-state running back in a huge all-male high school in Cleveland allayed any fears that a love of literature was only for girls. A Tom Tryon look alike, Collins was exceedingly handsome.

No one ever bolstered my self-worth as a student more than Dr. Sandra Driscoll at Aquinas College, when she defended me in a meeting with the academic dean, Father Charles Rooney, who was considering my case to remain on probation rather than be dismissed after another semester with a cumulative grade-point average below a 2.00. She had told me prior to the meeting, "Don't be intimidated by his feigned British accent; he's from Hazard, Kentucky." During my senior year, by then off academic probation, in her Shakespeare class, Dr. Driscoll wrote on one of my papers, "James, you have an uncommon facility for explicating literature. You should teach English." I did.

With his Miller Lite bottle empty, Jim O'Neill pulled the stapled donor envelope from the center of his copy of *Excalibur* and headed for his desk in the basement. He considered telling Maggie what he was thinking, but by this time she was snoring loudly. He sat down in his swivel, desk chair and thought about where his life might have gone had it not been for the teachers and institutions, for better or worse, that had shaped his perspective and taught him to synthesize information and experiences. Schools at every level were amalgamations of nearly myriad character shaping events and personalities, and the composite effect on a student was beyond difficult to measure or evaluate. Lasting impressions of mortifying moments and glowing successes competed for the psychological health of students throughout their lives. Had he, as a former teacher, been the agent of reassurance or frustration for his students? No teacher ever really knows how much he or she has impacted a student's life. Did he at any time destroy a student's confidence, or did he in the most unconscious manner say or do something that made him a Sister Lela Conroy, a Brother Jim Collins, or a Dr. Sandra Driscoll? He would likely never know. He withdrew his checkbook from his desk and started to write a $100.00 check to the Holy Cross High School Annual Fund, but he stopped and said, "Hell, I don't wanna be a grandstander," and wrote the check for $99.00.

The Shanachie

Write without pay until someone offers to pay.
If nobody offers within three years,
The candidate may look upon this circumstance
With the most implicit confidence
As a sign that sawing wood
Is what he was intended for.

—*The Atlantic*
Mark Twain

Michael Moran was only five or six years old the first time he gathered with the multitude of Moran Family cousins to listen to his paternal grandfather, Thomas Moran, on his Aunt Katy and Uncle Ed Kielty's farm in South Central Ohio. The 120-acre farm was Heaven-on-Earth for a boy, and while his helicopter mother held him in check as much as possible, he often found ways to sneak off with his two older brothers and four Kielty cousins to find devilment and adventure in barns, silos, cow-pens, and haylofts on the grounds; or gravel pit, railroad trestle, and drive-in theater within walking distance of the farm.

On any given weekend in the summer, most, if not all, of the children and grandchildren of Thomas J. and Ellen M. (Wynn) Moran gathered at the Kielty farm. When the sun went down, Grandpa Tom would seat himself at the end of one of the picnic tables in the old buggy barn and wrap himself around a vessel of draught beer tapped from one of the weekend kegs. Michael's father, John Francis Moran, was one of nine Moran children, four boys and five girls, and he and his siblings were all married now, practicing with hit-

and-miss precision the rhythm method of birth control, also known as Roman Roulette. "Fat Man" and "Little Boy" had ended World War II about five years before, and nearly all the sons and sons-in-law of Tom and Ellen had served in one of the branches of the military, several seeing action in the Pacific or European Theater. No matter how informal the consumption of hamburgers, baked beans, and corn-on-the-cob was in the buggy barn, no bread was broken until Grandma Ellen led the "Bless Us O Lord" prayer and gave heartfelt thanks to the Deity for bringing all the boys home from war. The pungent aroma of manure wafting from the hog pen across the lane, however, sometimes sullied the devotion. A particularly memorable night was on the occasion of the birthday of Michael's Aunt Mildred, the rather fastidious and urbane wife of Uncle Bob Moran. Ever the prankster, Uncle Ed Kielty had prepared a lovely gift-wrapped box containing Aunt Millie's birthday present. Having all sung the traditional happy birthday song; the cousins, aunts, and uncles gathered around Millie for the unveiling. There, under the box lid and wrapped in the purest white tissue paper, was the grandfather of all cow patties, and an engorged housefly seized the opportunity for a judicious escape. The shriek that Millie produced put a number of sows and piglets to run from their huts across the lane. Some uncles claimed that their ribs were still sore on Monday, but most of the aunts at least feigned a righteous indignation.

On such nights, Grandpa Tom, often in his cups, would transform into the consummate narrator and regale the grandkids with stories of Irish myths and legends. Fairy tales were supplemented with the exploits of Cuchulain of Muirthemne. Grandpa and Grandma Moran were immigrant Americans, having come "over on the boat" from County Sligo. As such, Grandpa Tom, much to the impatience of Grandma Ellen, was imbued with and happy to share the lore and legends of the Emerald Isle. He would lean forward on his elbows and become a Paddy Flynn, famous for his stories of the fairies, and, like Flynn, Grandpa Tom found little to admire about the fairies but loved to tell of them. While all the Moran Family cousins were fascinated by their grandfather's stories, for little Mikey Moran they were at the very genesis of his nascent passion to tell and write his own captivating tales.

Regardless of how many times he had provided the preamble, Grandpa Tom would always preface his first tale of the fairies with some folklore minutiae, as there might just be a grandchild or two who were not yet privy to this critical information.

"The Irish word for fairies," he would begin with still a hint of that Sligo lilt, "is 'sheehogue,' and dependin' on whom ya believe, they were fallen angels who weren't holy enough to remain in Heaven but not so bad they deserved roastin' in the fires of hell. Some folks are as sure that the Irish are God's chosen people that the fairies are the gods of the Earth. If ya please 'em, they'll do their best to protect ya, but if ya don't, beware! But every true Irishman knows that the fairies are not always small. They can make themselves any size or into any form that suits 'em. They've got three festivals each year, and the one they'd be celebratin' about now would be the festival of Midsummer's Eve. That's when they're at their happiest and sometimes run away with our beautiful girls and make 'em their brides, the sneaky bas..., uh scoundrels."

Grandpa Tom would likely begin a story with something like this: "I don't know if I've ever told ya about the priest's supper. Well, it seems the fairies or gnomes, the 'good people' as they liked to be called, were playin' some of their pranks on a moonlit night in September in County Cork. On the green sod of the river bank, they were dancin' and cavortin' until one of 'em cries out, 'Cease, cease, with your drumming, here's an end to our mumming; by my smell, I can tell a priest is this way coming.' They all ran off and hid themselves among the stones and crannies.

"Soon, Father Horrigan approached on his horse, and, since the hour was late, he decided to stop at the nearby cottage of Dermod Leary. As Father Horrigan was greatly loved and revered among the people of Inchegeela, Dermod was woefully regretful that all he and his wife could offer the good priest was a boiled potato. He remembered, however, that he'd set his net about an hour earlier in the hope of catchin' a nice salmon, so dashin' from his cottage, he ran to the bank of the river but with little hope a snarin' a fish so soon. Pullin' the net from the river, he found a magnificent salmon he could offer the saintly priest. As he grasped the net to retrieve the fish, it was pulled back so violently into the river that the beautiful salmon swam easily out of reach and merrily on his way. 'Curse you fish!' cried Dermod.   'Only the devil himself would free you and deny a holy priest a fine meal.'

"Respondin' to Dermod's angry denunciation, one of the fairies emerged and said, 'That's not true. There was only a dozen or so of us pulling on your net. If you'd like a fine meal for your priest, go back and ask him a question for us, and he'll have such a meal before him in no time at all.'

"Dermod, of course, wanted nothin' to do with these shameful fairies, and so he replied, 'Father Horrigan would never want me to make a deal with the likes of you just for a better meal.'

"The spokesman for the fairies persisted, 'All that we seek is that you ask a polite question.'

"Dermod relented and said, 'What's your question?'

"With all the others crowdin' in, the speakin' fairy said, 'Ask Father Horrigan if our souls will be saved like all the good Christians.'

"Dermod just about flew back to the cottage and asked the priest the question on behalf of the fairies, but the sage and kindly man of God replied, 'Go tell them to come here and ask me themselves, and then I'll be happy to answer their question.'

"When Dermod arrived back at the bank and gave the fairies the priest's response, they bolted and fled like a herd of impala bein' chased by a lion. Dermod was astonished by the fact that this humble priest, who'd have only a potato for supper, could banish such a number of fairies by his words alone."

Hearing the end of one of Grandpa Tom's stories, the kids would always petition for more, and depending upon the hour, he was not loath to accommodate them.

"Well, there is one I like about a devil cat."

"Tell us, tell us!" came the response. Mikey was ever so pleased that there was enough strength in numbers to win Grandpa Tom's acquiescence. After one of the kids fetched him another schooner of beer, he continued.

"As the story goes, a woman in Connacht Province was especially skilled at catchin' fish, and she'd store 'em up to take to market, but whenever she was ready to take 'em to the town square, a huge black cat would come in the night and devour the biggest and best fish. She resolved to wait on this blasted cat and beat it with a cudgel.

"Shortly thereafter, she and a friend were arrangin' fish together in her kitchen when the monstrous cat burst through the door hissin' and growlin'. When the friend screamed that the cat must be a devil, the vicious feline turned and raked her across the face with his claws and then did the same to the fisherwoman. Hearin' their screamin' in pain from their gapin' wounds, a passin' tinker, a fellow who mends pots and pans, pushed in the door to provide some assistance. He was immediately attacked by the giant cat and sent howlin' in misery from the claw and teeth wounds on his face, hands, and arms.

"The ferocious cat then pranced past the cowerin' women and began eatin' the best fish they had laid out for market. Angered by his bold intrusions and wicked attacks, the two women grabbed tongs and pokers from the fireplace and began beatin' the cat fiercely but to no avail. He in turn attacked 'em again, this time so savagely the bloodied women were barely able to escape the house and appeal for help.

"A passin' priest stopped and listened to their horror story and handed the fisherwoman a vile of holy water. Said he to the terrorized victim, 'Take this and sprinkle the water on the evil feline, good woman, and your cat woes will be over.'

"Creepin' into the house, the woman approached the maraudin' cat from behind and sprinkled the holy water on his back. The cat began shriekin', and the smell of smoke and brimstone filled the house. The cat disintegrated slowly to a cinder and then to just a dark spot on the floor. The devilish gnome in the form of a cat would decimate the woman's fish catch no more."

As the years passed, Michael would hear many more of Grandpa Tom's tales of fairies, involving the likes of jackdaws, giants, kings, queens, witches, horned women, tainted butter, and hexed cows; and with each passing summer, he became more intrigued with his grandfather's story-telling prowess. When Grandpa Tom told of the legends of Cuchulain, who Michael decided was Ireland's Boewulf, his descriptive powers cast the die of his grandson's professional hopes.

Michael Moran would hang on every expressive word or phrase, as his grandfather recounted such events as Cuchulain's birth, the Cattle Raid of Cooley, and Cuchulain's death. Grandpa Tom's sheer joy in the telling of a story was contagious for Michael, and the memory of it long after his grandfather passed would sustain him for a time in his own efforts, even when a dearth of inspiration or writer's block would be maddening.

Neither the shenanigans of fairies nor the heroics of Cuchulain, however, held such sway over Michael Moran's life like his grandfather's testimony of his own father that Grandpa Tom shared with his grandson privately some weeks before the old narrator's death.

"My da was a strappin' young man of about twenty when he was comin' home after another long day a cuttin' peat from the raised bogs. As he made his way carefully through the bog fields that were much like quicksand in places, he heard the screams of a woman, and she was hollerin', 'Help us! Help me husband! Help us someone, please!' My da ran over a bluff and saw a woman holdin' an infant girl and tryin' desperately to extend her coat to a man who was by this time with only his right arm and head above one of those cursed bog holes. Da ran down to the edge of the bog hole, where the poor fellow had probably less than a minute before he disappeared, and told the woman to lay the girl down and then hold his booted feet while he extended himself as far as he could to the seemingly doomed husband. With all his prodigious strength, Da spent the next half-hour pullin' the fella inch-by-inch out of the bog.

"Covered in mud and exhausted, both men embraced each other like brothers while the wife of the saved man wept with joy and thanked Da profusely. After some introductions and expressions of good will, the man and woman and child departed from Da where he had sat down to rest himself. Now nearly pitch dark and growin' colder by the minute, Da rose to his feet to continue his trek home. As he was reachin' for his cap, he looked up to see a beautiful boy surrounded by an aura with his hand extended toward Da.

"The boy held in his hand an elaborate box and within it a gold medallion, and handin' the box to Da, he explained, 'This is your reward for a selfless act of bravery that saved the life of a young husband and father.' As Da took the box in hand, the boy disappeared. When Da returned to my grandfather and grandmother's cottage, he opened the box and found the gold medallion. In the candlelight, Da saw the traditional Irish Claddagh with the hands, heart, and crown on one side and an inscription on the reverse side: 'If you are good and true to yourself, you will always be blessed.' "

When Grandpa Tom finished the story of his father and the medallion, he drew Michael closer to him with his furrowed hand and said softly, "Mikey, I've always known that you love good tales and hope to be a writer of fascinatin' stories. For that reason, I wantta give ya somethin'."

Grandpa Tom went to a desk and withdrew an ornate box, and then said, "Mikey, this is the box that was given to my da by the beautiful and mysterious boy on that fateful night in the bogs. Da gave it to me many years ago, and I've tried to live my life by the words within." He handed it to Michael, and said, "Open it."

When Michael opened the box, he found, of course, the gold medallion, vividly inscribed.

"I want ya to have it, and let the words guide ya in your life and your aspirations."

Michael Moran treasured the gift like no other he would ever receive, and though his Grandfather Moran would soon pass, Michael resolved to live his life as the medallion suggested and his grandfather had hoped.

Michael followed the script for a good Catholic boy in the fifties and sixties. He developed his reading and reasoning skills in grade school and committed to memory all the responses to the Latin Mass in his successful pursuit of selection as an altar boy. Sports became a way of life for him, and he played Catholic Youth Organization football, basketball, and baseball in grade school. Attending the huge all-male and Catholic Saint Aloysius High School, he was able to make only the football team, on which he became an enthusiastic and above average defensive back.

As a high school student, Michael studied hard, often overcoming certain academic weaknesses with perspiration, protracted study, and teacher assistance; trigonometry and its attendant annoyance, the slide rule, being particularly mind numbing. He excelled naturally, however, in Latin and French and could always read and memorize his way to success in history and government classes. His English classes were easily his first love and provided his most enjoyable studies. In his senior year, he borrowed some of his grandfather's blarney and lore, and he submitted a short story to the local newspaper that won first prize for the fiction category and earned him $250.00 (which he blew on movies, dates, and clothes). As graduation approached, Michael, like virtually every one of his classmates in his academically elite high school, was thinking of the presumed sequence of experiences: college.   With Notre Dame his dream, his parents' financial resources came nowhere near affording the hefty costs under the Golden Dome. At a College Night in March at Saint Aloysius, Michael drifted across the gymnasium floor and found himself at the display table for John Carroll University. Having no real interest in the school, he picked up a glossy brochure and was greeted by a young man in a blue blazer, white shirt, and gold tie and armed with a huge smile.

"What are ya looking for in a school?"

Mike laughed and said, "Notre Dame, but there's no point in applying. The tuition is way beyond what my parents and I can afford."

"You've just said the magic words," the engaging young man said with a disarming laugh. "As we say in University Heights, 'If ya can't go ta Notre Dame, come to John Carroll.' "

"Whatya mean?"

Extending his hand, the Carroll recruiter said, "I'm Tom Callahan, and John Carroll is really just a downsized Notre Dame, without the Golden Dome, of course. We do have a magnificent bell tower, though, that's just as impressive as the dome." He winked and smiled. "Do you have a major in mind?"

"Yeah. I'm pretty sure I wanna major in English."

"Didya play any sports here at Aloysius?"

"Yeah. Football for four years."

"Bingo on both counts!"

"Why's that?"

"We have a terrific English Department, headed by the illustrious Father Savage, and the Blue Streaks always need football talent. I played myself for four years."

Mike Moran was toast. Tom Callahan was a recent John Carroll graduate and one of the assistant admissions directors. He was the perfect recruiter: handsome but not pretty, articulate but not flowery, and gregarious but not suffocating. Callahan gave Mike some dates when he would be on campus and available to provide a very personalized college visit. Mike applied, and after receiving his acceptance letter, he took Callahan up on a visit to John Carroll. After a tour of the beautiful Collegiate Gothic campus and a very encouraging meeting with the football coach, Mike came home and told his parents he was heading for John Carroll in early August, when he would begin two-a-days with the football team. He spent June and July washing tableware in the dish and pan rooms at nearby Ursula Hospital to earn as much of his tuition as possible, and then he leaned on his mom and dad for the remainder.

Things went well for Mike Moran at John Carroll, where he was able to mature intellectually and socially. Although football took much of his time and left him exhausted as he headed to the study carrels of Grasselli Library in the evenings to write papers or cram for tests, he enjoyed his classes so thoroughly he made the dean's list in both semesters and received a nearly full academic scholarship for the next three years.

Applying to the Boston College, Marquette University, Xavier University, and Miami University graduate schools for master's degree work in English, the easy choice for him became Miami University because of its breathtaking sylvan setting and gorgeous buildings and trees, but mostly because Miami offered him a full assistantship with stipend for his two-year program.

Quite often during his undergraduate years at John

Carroll, Mike would take out the gold medallion and remind himself of its guidance: "If you are good and true to yourself, you will always be blessed." It buoyed him in times of discouragement.

In mid January of his second year at Miami, Mike was busy one cold night contributing to the health of Oxford commerce at Mac 'n Joe's Bar on North High Street. Turning from the bar with his second frothy mug of draught beer, he collided with another student and spilled at least half of the mug's golden contents down the front of her blouse.

The student's reaction was swift and spontaneous, "You jackass!"

Michael Moran had never seen a girl so angry and so beautiful at the same time. Given where he had spilled the beer, he could only watch as she used a bar towel to wipe and dry a satiny gray blouse that was tucked smartly into a pair of very tight, black stirrup pants, the waistline of which was also drenched.

"Hey, I'm sorry! I didn't see you when I was turnin' around. I'll be glad to pay for any dry cleaning. Can I buy ya a beer?"

"You can get the hell out of her face," said a guttural voice next to him belonging to a man-mountain that was with the girl and about whom Mike would be informed shortly by the bartender.

"Uh, sure! But I would like to pay for any cleaning."

At this point, the girl turned to her protector and said, "Jim, it's all right. I know it was an accident." To Mike, she said, "You don't have to pay for the dry cleaning. Most of what I wear in here smells like beer anyway."

She smiled warmly and then walked over to a table with her brawny escort to join some other students. The bartender tapped on Mike's shoulder and said, "That's Janice Warner, and she's a senior in education. She's in here a lot. The big stud she's with is Jim Smithson, who's been a back-up tackle on the Miami football team."

Mike smiled sarcastically and said, "Since he played for Miami, I guess I won't hafta go over there and hurt 'im."

"Yeah, right. Janice is damned pretty, though!"

"Pretty" was an adjective that hardly did Janice Warner justice. Her jet-black hair was cut short but with bangs that made her seem childlike. Her brown eyes dominated a gorgeous face, and at about 5'8", her athletic figure featured legs and buns would have sold gobs of women's jeans for any manufacturer.

"Really? I hardly noticed."

"Well, in case ya do notice, I think she lives in Talawanda Hall if you'd like ta make amends."

"Why ya tellin' me this? You think I'd have a chance with her?"

"Maybe. She's really a nice kid, but the guy she's with's a jerk. A real loudmouth who bullies a lot of people. If he was any good, he wouldn't a been a backup for four years."

"Thanks for the information. I may risk my young life and see if I can make some inroads."

Moran had completed the thirty-semester-hour coursework for his Master of Arts in English in December, and he would now devote the winter term to the six-semester-hour thesis requirement. Departing from the traditional research-paper thesis, he had asked for and been granted the permission to write a novel to meet his degree requirements. A Miami graduate committee rarely approved such a proposal for a thesis.

To meet his stipend obligations, Moran had been teaching one section of Composition 101 or 102 each semester, and the current semester was no different. The work also prepared him somewhat for a distant-second plan as a college instructor if he could not make a living as a writer. The more immediate problem, however, was the writer's block that was preventing any meaningful grist for a novel. No amount of reflection or library searching suggested any theme worth pursuing. He could, of course, take up to five years to complete the master's requirements, but he had no interest in being on campus beyond the summer. In the meantime, he had a better fish to catch, and that fish was living in Talawanda Hall. The problem was the bait. He decided that he would simply drop an apology note off at the desk for Janice with a carefully written and totally innocent offer.

The content of the message was most eloquent: "Sorry I baptized you with suds the other night, but if you'd like to experience another dose of Irish charm and éclat over dinner, give me a call.—Mike Moran." Under his message, Mike had written his telephone number and the address of his small apartment at the edge of Oxford. He left the note at the reception desk at Talawanda. The young woman working the desk asked, "Would you like me to ring her room?"

"No. I don't live my life that dangerously."

She laughed and said, "I'll see personally that she gets the note, Casanova."

When he was not teaching comp or grading papers, Moran was in and out of King Library reading microfilm and following up some rather lame ideas for a novel. February was now upon him, and he was still stuck in first gear. Arriving at his very modest digs around 10:30 p.m. one night, he knew he would still have to grade at least six essays to meet the daily quota he had set for himself. He reached in his mailbox and found the usual junk mail, but his fingers touched a loose piece of paper stuffed at the bottom of the chute. When he plopped into an old stuffed chair, probably used by William Holmes McGuffey, he pulled the table lamp chain and found a note: "Hey, graceful! I got your invitation and did a little checking on you. If you've got the money for dinner, I'll take a chance on you.—Janice"

Only then did Mike check the note more closely, and its date was for four days earlier. Now Tuesday, he hopped in his car and ran a response note down to Talawanda Hall and left it at the desk. It said: "I'll pick you up here at 7:00 Friday evening and we'll go to dinner. Two requirements: First, don't decline; and second, look as good as you did at Mac 'n Joe's.—Mike"

On Friday night, Mike had to wait about fifteen minutes at the desk for Janice to come downstairs. His fears that she had changed her mind were completely allayed when he saw her on the stairs in a pleated white skirt and a black blouse.

"Have you been waiting long?"

"Yeah!"

"Good!"

They went for spaghetti at a small Italian restaurant outside Oxford and talked nearly nonstop. By the time Mike got around to his thesis dilemma, they both had pretty much learned the other's life story. Janice was a Miami girl through and through, but her father was actually a Colonel in the United States Army and the head of the R.O.T.C. program at Ohio University.

"Boy, I've really hit a wall with the novel I need to write for my thesis."

"Well, I'm not Irish, of course, but why don't you tie it to some of that Irish family history you have?"

"Naah! Who'd be interested in that?"

"Well, I was just now as you were telling me about it."

After dinner, they went back to Mike's apartment and began what would become the most vitalizing time of Michael Moran's life. Janice practically lived there until her graduation in June. During those months, Mike worked feverishly on his novel that he would call *The Shanachie*. It would blend a fictionalized account of his grandfather's life in Ireland and America with his own journey to becoming an accomplished writer of stories.

One early-May afternoon, Janice, who now had her own key to the apartment, let herself in while Mike was at his desk grading some essays to return to students the next day. She was clearly crestfallen and discouraged.

"Well, that didn't go very well!"

She was talking about the interview she had just had with the principal and two teachers at Englewood Elementary regarding a fourth grade teaching position.

"Why's that?"

"I'm not sure. I think I answered all their questions thoroughly, but I don't think one of the teachers cared very much for my candor."

"Really! Poor baby. Maybe everybody in the world doesn't think that just because you're sexy you're a good teacher."

She smacked him on the back of the head.

"Lemme show ya something."

Mike went to his top dresser drawer and withdrew from a sock the small box containing the gold medallion. He had never before shown it to anyone outside the family. He opened the box and handed Janice the medallion.

"That's a claddagh."

"I know what it is, Dopey."

"Read the back to me out loud."

Turning the medallion, Janice read the inscription aloud, " 'If you are good and true to yourself, you will always be blessed.' "

"I think you must've been good 'n true to yourself today. You may not get that job, but if you follow those words, you're gonna get a good one."

"You think so, huh! Just because you believe in this?"

"Yeah, and because my grandfather gave it to me, but mostly because I've got a serious case a the hots for your ass."

"You're no damned good, ya know that?"

"Yeah, but I'm real lovable."

About a week later, Janice Warner was called back for a second interview for the Englewood position, and, following the session, the principal offered her the job on the spot. At graduation in June, Janice not only had her Bachelor of Science in Elementary Education, but also a contract to teach fourth grade at Englewood Elementary.

Although pleased with Janice's success, Mike Moran began to feel some desperation in regard to his own graduation and subsequent livelihood. Janice had gone home to Athens, Ohio for most of the summer, although she returned to Oxford periodically and stayed with Mike while spending a day or two at nearby Englewood Elementary School, preparing her classroom and gathering teaching materials. By the end of July, Mike was closing in on the completion of *The Shanachie* and was nearly ready to present the manuscript to his graduate committee in time to meet an August graduation deadline.

Janice Warner was back in Athens when Michael Moran was standing outside one of the conference rooms in McGuffey Hall on that hot day in August. He nervously clutched the manila folder that held his own copy of the draft of *The Shanachie*. It was a pretty impressive first novel, he believed. That belief was, nevertheless, scant comfort to him as he awaited his summoning to the "slings and arrows" that English scholars Dr. James Schwieterman, Dr. Jan Bradley, and Dr. John Tennley (his advisor) would visit upon the results of his past seven months of tedious and exasperating efforts.

At length, Dr. Tennley emerged from what Mike anticipated would be the academic equivalent of a Spanish Inquisition chamber. Mike's interpretation of Tennley's polite salutation was tantamount to " 'Welcome to my parlor,' said the spider to the unwary fly." Noting Moran's anxieties, Tennley tried to assuage his fears, telling him to relax, take some deep breaths, and bear in mind that he had written the novel, not the committee. Re-entering the conference room, he said over his shoulder, "Remember, you're the expert."

Easy for him to say, Mike thought.

When Dr. Tennley opened the door again, he brought Mike before the tribunal that would decide his fate. All three committee members held copies of his thesis/novel as they began their review of the manuscript. Mike breezed through the queries of Dr. Schwieterman and Dr. Tennley, asserting himself with the confidence his advisor had encouraged. With the brass ring nearly in Mike's grasp, Dr. Bradley withdrew from her folder a legal-sized note pad with two or three pages of questions. Boring in with probing and salient inquiries, she gave Mike to think he was doomed by his failure to have scrutinized or clarified just one more detail or element. Dismissed from the room, he awaited his judgment. In a matter of minutes, Dr. Tennley summoned him to the conference room where a committee that had made only perfunctory recommendations for revisions warmly congratulated Michael Moran.

Practically floating to his car, Mike reflected on what had just happened. Never mind what the degree would or would not generate in professional success; for the moment, at least, he would simply revel in his imminent Master of Arts in English from staid old Miami University.

With summer over and the euphoria of completing his master's beginning to fade, Michael had to face reality. He was well educated but unemployed. He found a listing for an adjunct, composition instructor at the University of Cincinnati in the Miami University placement bulletin. What he really wanted, of course, was to be a published writer, and toward that end he began paging daily through the *Writer's Market* that listed virtually every publishing house in America and included a profile of what each company sought in genre, style, and theme. He sent a cover letter over a resume to the U.C. English Department Chair, and within two days received a call asking for a meeting. The salary was based on a per-class basis, and the chairwoman needed him for three sections of Composition 101. He accepted the job immediately for three reasons: he had no alternative; he would have time to submit his novel and query letter to selected publishing houses; and Cincinnati was fairly close to Englewood Elementary in Southwestern Ohio.

In the meantime, Mike was beginning to fear that Janice would drift away from him now that she was fully employed and in every way the epitome of the stylish and beautiful young teacher. She had taken an apartment in a new complex on Route 73 near Englewood Elementary and was furnishing it with items from her parents' home and some new things she was picking up herself. Mike helped her move in, and on the Friday night before her first day of classes, they split a bottle of wine and a pizza. Mike knew that he would never find another girl like Janice. She was perfect for him.

Mike had taken a furnished apartment near the U.C. campus and Burnett Woods. It was not elegant, but it was affordable on his meager salary. His classes went well, and the full-time instructors greeted him kindly each day. Although his assignment had the shades of a grad assistant's status, he would have really settled into the pleasure of interacting with bright young people if he had not been absolutely obsessed with being a published writer. Would giving up on that dream be a betrayal of the words on his medallion and the faith that his grandfather had in him? He simply would not allow it.

While Janice's career had taken off like a rocket, Mike's was in Limbo. Even Janice's principal remarked to the superintendent that there was a quantum leap in the number of the fourth-graders' fathers who attended the open house and parent conferences. For Mike, each week brought another rejection letter or two from a publisher that had more than likely tossed his manuscript for *The Shanachie* on to the slush pile. Imagining that Janice was now seeing other guys, his jealousy grew and his phone calls to her were more and more caustic. An evening out on a weekend typically ended in an argument based on his veiled accusations of her disinterest in him.

Although Mike of necessity remained sober and clear-headed during the week, he began drinking so heavily on weekends that he could no longer afford even his modest flat near the U.C. campus. Forced by circumstances, he down-graded to a furnished efficiency in a dilapidated, five-story tenement house in the Over-the-Rhine district near the Mill Creek Express. By this time, Janice had lost track of him, as he had told no one of his humiliating move. He had, of course, no telephone service at home, only a phone booth about a half-block down the street that frequently had the receiver and cord ripped from the box.

As his doubts about his life's achievements increased, Mike frequently reflected upon his absence from military service during the unrelenting Vietnam War. Yes, his draft board had exempted full-time students and teachers at any instructional level, but his father and two brothers had served their country honorably in the U.S. Armed Services. His dad had been a captain in the Army Air Corps during World War II. His older brother had been a Specialist-4 in the Army Signal Corps during the Berlin Crisis; and his old-est brother, a West Point graduate, had just returned from a year in Vietnam, serving as a captain in the Army Combat Engineers. With more time now to ponder and lament his non-service, he was full of self-reproach.

What troubled Mike almost more than anything in his daily routine, however, was the presence of a strikingly diminutive fellow whose apartment was directly across the hall from his on the third floor of the building. He was no more than 4'10" tall with a rather disturbing countenance and build. So annoyed by the unattractive fellow was Mike that when he passed him in the hall or stairway, he refused to speak to him in spite of his neighbor's polite greetings and efforts to communicate. On Friday and Saturday nights, after closing up the bar down the block, Mike would stagger up the stoop outside the building and then somehow navi-gate the three flights to his apartment door. Invariably, his little neighbor would open his door to offer assistance, only to be cursed and verbally abused by Mike before he fell into his apartment.

This sober-during-the-week and drunk-on-the-weekends routine was reinforced by a series of rejection letters from publishing houses and the agonizing and reasonable belief that he had destroyed any relationship with Janice. His only real comfort was the increasing delight he was taking in his teaching, but the quarter seemed to be racing toward its conclusion in December and quite possibly the end of his adjunct assignment at U.C. He had had a few brief conversations with his department chair in her office about the possibilities for the second quarter, but she had been rather noncommittal. She had been most supportive and had brought no complaints to his attention, but she seemed to play all decisions close to the vest.

On the Friday night before the last week of the quarter in December, Michael Moran had reached an all-time low. He withdrew the box with the medallion from a bureau by his bed and pondered the inscription: "If you are good and true to yourself, you will always be blessed."

"I don't think so, Grandpa! I don't think so!"

Mike put the medallion in his shirt pocket; pulled into a sleeveless, goose-down jacket; and headed down the stairs for another night of boozing. Upon his return around 3:00 a.m., he collapsed at the bottom of the staircase in a drunken stupor. Several residents stepped over or kicked him as they climbed the stairs before the gnome-like gentleman across the hall found him, and with extraordinary strength he carried Michael up three flights of stairs to his apartment door, where, finding the key in his neighbor's jacket pocket, he laid his burden on the couch and covered him with a blanket. Waking about an hour later, Mike reached for the medallion in his shirt pocket, only to find it gone.

Panicked even in his drunken condition, he shouted at the Good Samaritan seated in a chair across from him, "Where's my medallion, and how did I get here?"

"I carried you up and laid you on the couch. You were unconscious on the stairs, three flights down."

"Why do you treat me so kindly? I've never given you a civil word."

"Perhaps my purpose is to look after you and the medallion. In any case, it will turn up in time."

"I don't know why I treasure it so. I've been good and true to myself in my hopes to be a professional writer, but look at me. My grandfather was wrong and the medallion is wrong. I've worked so hard to read and study the masters and share their passion, but what am I but a glorified schoolmarm? My grandfather was wrong!"

"When your grandfather told you to live by the message of the medallion, perhaps he meant for you to be true to yourself by sharing your love of the written word with the young men and women you teach."

"Oh, hell, I don't know anymore. And I don't give a damn!"

With that, Mike lay back on the couch again and fell into a restless, alcohol-induced sleep. In that sleep, he dreamt of a beautiful young boy, smiling at him and extending his hand that held the box and medallion.

Before he left Michael Moran's roach-infested apartment, the gnome-man replaced the medallion in the box on the bureau. The medallion had been under Mike on the bottom step, having fallen from his shirt pocket when he slumped to the stairs. He left the apartment and the tenement house, and he never returned.

In the morning, Michael came slowly to his senses and his recollection of the previous night. Instinctively, he looked in the box and found the medallion. He relieved himself, washed his face, and walked across the hall to talk to his neighbor. Knocking several times, he surmised intuitively that his Good Samaritan had left for good. He did not care. He would tell him anyway. "I want you to know that I believe you found my medallion and that you're right about my teaching. I've lost the girl that I love and probably a career as a writing teacher, but if I get another chance, I won't blow it. Thank you, my good and caring neighbor!"

On Monday, Mike Moran found a note in his mailbox from his department chair, simply saying, "See me, ASAP." He went directly to her office, thinking some kind of complaint had been made against him for something he had said or done while drunk over the weekend.

"Mike, I'm gonna need someone to teach one section of Comp 101 and two sections of Comp 102 in the spring quarter. Do ya want 'em?"

"You're damned right! Er, of course!"

"I've also just been granted the funding by the dean for additional summer instructors and for a non-tenure track, full-time comp instructor in the fall for the entire year. Would ya like those too?"

"You're kiddin'."

"Nope!"

"Will I have my own office?"

She leaned forward and laughed derisively. "Don't push it. You'll share one."

"You've got me. You don't know how much this means to me!"

"Yes, I do. I've been where you are. Go teach young man, go teach."

On Friday afternoon, after Mike had turned in his grades, he stopped at the office of his old apartment complex near campus to check on unit vacancies. There would be one opening the next Friday, but if he did not have to have it cleaned before he moved in, he could have it on Monday, with a six-month lease. He took it. He decided to return to the office he shared with another adjunct and use the desk phone. With his heart in his throat, he dialed the number.

"Hello."

"I was just wonderin' if you'd like to have dinner tonight with a full-time instructor at the University of Cincinnati, who tends to slop his beer a bit."

There was no response.

"Hey, are you there?"

A heaving voice finally answered. "Of course, I'm here, you jackass!"

"Well, I..."

"Yes, I'll have dinner with you tonight on two conditions: One, you get here by seven 'cause I'm starvin'; and two, you're as sorry as you were for your performance at Mac 'n Joe's."

"Close your eyes. I'll be there when ya open 'em."

John Hagan was born in Presque Isle, Maine, and shortly thereafter his family returned to Dayton, Ohio, where he was reared and educated.

Retiring from a career as a high school English teacher and secondary school administrator, he was hired as an adjunct, composition instructor at The University of Dayton, where he taught for six years. Interacting with college students in the classroom and grading their essays and research papers, John gained significant insight into the current thinking of young adults.

Leaving U.D. for total retirement from education, John now spends much of his time between his home in Springboro, Ohio and his labor of love, a forty-acre horse farm in Highland County, Ohio. "Down on the farm," he divides his energies among field and barn work, horseback riding, bridle trail running, and poem and short-story writing. His days at the farm with his Border Collies and Quarter Horses have influenced much of his writing.

John earned undergraduate and graduate degrees in English and secondary school administration at Thomas More University, Xavier University, and Miami University.